I0544161

THICKER THAN THIEVES

THE TRAVELERS: BOOK EIGHT

MICHAEL P. KING

BLURRED LINES PRESS

Blurred Lines Press

Thicker Than Thieves

Michael P. King

ISBN 978-1-952711-00-8

Copyright © 2020 by Michael P. King

All rights reserved

Cover design by Paramita Bhattacharjee at creativeparamita.com

Thicker Than Thieves is a work of fiction. The names, characters, places, and events are products of the author's imagination or are used fictitiously. Any similarity to real persons or places is entirely coincidental.

"King's fans will relish this smoothly set up con that, like others in the series, has just enough complexity to allow unexpected chaos to occur.... His nuanced antiheroes steal the show.... This entry's mellow finale, memorable cast, and emotional weight may have readers hoping for a direct sequel. That said, the author rarely offers reader what they expect."—*Kirkus Reviews*

Mob diamonds, white nationalists, and Middle Eastern jihadis ...

On the prowl to steal a crime cartel's diamond shipment, the Travelers zero in on the smugglers—an Iranian American pair of brother and sister oriental carpet importers. They have twelve weeks to manipulate the smugglers, figure out the details of the diamond delivery, and escape with the diamonds without tipping off the cartel.

But Middle Eastern jihadis hoping to create chaos in the US and white nationalists intent on a terrorist act bigger than the 1995 Oklahoma City bombing also have plans for the smugglers.

And when the FBI gets wind of these plots, the Travelers' plans are suddenly careening sideways....

Thicker Than Thieves is a roller-coaster ride through a mine field of danger and conspiracy. If you like mind-boggling suspense, unpredictable plot twists, and criminal intrigue, you'll love the eighth novel in the Travelers series.

For Sarah

1

POINTS OF ENTRY

The Travelers, now going by the names Danny and Genie Briggs, sat in lounge chairs on their private balcony at the Spice Islands Retreat in the Florida Keys. Danny was in his early fifties, slightly over six feet, with an athletic build and a face that was hard to remember. When he spoke, what he said somehow always seemed right. Genie was in her early forties, but passed for late thirties. She had the looks of a lead in a romance movie. And yet their marks always somehow seemed to believe that they deserved to be with her.

Danny and Genie had been enjoying the last few months of vacation, but now they were down to their next-job planning money. They needed a new scam, one that would pay. They'd been calling contacts over the last few days—ten percenters—people who found opportunities and sold them for part of the payout. Some jobs didn't pay enough, and some jobs were too dangerous coming out of the gate. And because they only robbed criminals, some jobs didn't fit their MO. But now they were talking with Billy on speakerphone. He was their one-stop shop for equipment and specialists, and he had a job that had piqued their interest.

"So this is up the East Coast?" Danny asked.

"Mid-Atlantic."

The breeze came up, fluttering Genie's silk robe. She smoothed it down and adjusted the belt. "Run through it again."

"Okay," Billy said. "The Orange Hill Cartel brings in diamonds twice a year. Always ten million dollars. They smuggle them in with a shipment of oriental carpets routed out of Mumbai."

"Mumbai? Isn't there a diamond trading hub near there?" Genie asked.

"You got it."

"And the shipment always comes from there?"

"Twice a year."

Danny ran his hand over his gray-streaked beard. "And this carpet shipment always goes to the same carpet wholesaler?"

"They take a container of carpets every six weeks, so it mixes right in."

"So ten million retail. That's what? Two million five hundred at the cash-converters' price with the right paperwork."

"You won't have the paperwork."

Genie cut in. "So we're really talking around one hundred thousand cash from a fence or a crooked diamond distributor."

"Give or take," Billy said.

"And the carpet wholesalers?"

"The Hashemis. Brother and sister. Inherited the business from their father."

"Immigrants?"

"Born here, raised here. Their father came from Iran."

"Iran?" Danny asked.

"Yeah, but they call themselves Persian. It's a political thing. They've got a legit business."

"So smuggling is their sideline?"

"Appears to be."

"And you're sure of which shipment?"

"Yes. About twelve weeks from now, they'll get the fall shipment with the diamonds."

"How do you know the diamonds aren't taken out of the container before it's delivered?" Genie asked.

"My info's good."

Danny glanced at Genie. She nodded. "Drop all the particulars into the usual cloud account," Danny said. "If they check out, we're in."

Later, after supper, they sat against the headboard of their bed in their underwear, a laptop computer resting on Danny's thighs, looking over the information that Billy had sent. Eskander "Zander" Hashemi and Nadia Hashemi Wright, owners of Hashemi Wholesale Carpets & Arts.

"They don't look like foreigners," Genie said.

Danny zoomed in on the picture. Zander Hashemi was a thin, dark-haired man with a closely cropped beard who could have passed for almost anyone from the Mediterranean. His sister was a curvy, almond-eyed beauty with long, dark hair. "You heard what Billy said. They're second generation. So they're just dark-skinned Americans with unusual holidays."

"She's a good-looking woman."

Danny grinned. "And she's a widow. Makes my job easier."

"If she's not still pining."

"Husband's been dead a few years. The newspaper clipping— reading between the lines—looks like he might have got killed in a turf war."

"So you think they're part-timers who are in over their heads?"

"Looks that way."

"If you're going to seduce her, I'll need a different last name."

"What have you got in mind?"

"I've already got the Genie Pullman ID." Genie reached over to the laptop computer to scroll down. "All the action is at the Port of Point Jericho."

"Specialty container port. That's good for us. Containers moving in and out all day long and not nearly enough port cops to keep an eye on things."

"It'll be the usual union setup," Genie continued. "Probably lots of guys coming and going. Remember the scam at the Port of Long Beach? It was a license to print money."

"That was a beautiful job. We need to find a service we can offer at Point Jericho."

"Wonder if the Hashemis have any other action going on?"

"Would make things easier." Danny closed the laptop. "So?"

"If we can stay out of the way of the Orange Hill mob," Genie replied, "this looks like our kind of job."

"Then let's do it."

TWO WEEKS LATER, Danny and Genie walked into the lunchtime crowd at the Blue Rose Bar and Grill in Point Jericho. Danny was clean shaven. He wore a gray suit with no tie. Genie wore a low-cut sweater and tight slacks, her auburn hair dancing around her shoulders as she scanned the room. The restaurant was noisy with conversation. Two men and a woman, all three in business wear, were waiting at the hostess station. Danny and Genie squeezed past them.

Genie put her hand on Danny's shoulder. "Back corner."

He turned his head. There they were, sitting on one side of a booth at the far wall, Zander Hashemi and Nadia Hashemi Wright.

Zander noticed them and waved. Danny smiled and nodded. He and Genie made their way through the tables to the booth and slid in opposite them.

"Would you care for some lunch?" Zander asked. "The food here is good."

"Coffee will be fine," Genie said. She shifted her weight to call attention to her cleavage, but Zander wasn't looking.

Nadia motioned to their server. The server brought menus for Danny and Genie. "Just coffee for us," Danny said.

The server walked away. Danny turned to Zander and Nadia. "You ready to talk business?"

Zander shrugged. "We've checked you out, so we won't insult you by asking if you're wearing a wire."

"Same here," Danny replied.

"But we're not going to get into our business. Our need is simple—"

The server returned with the coffees. After she left, Nadia picked up the thread. "Sometimes we need a container moved from the port."

Genie smiled. "We thought you were with the cartel."

"We are, but some things we do on our own."

"And," Zander continued, "we currently need an inside man."

"We know a guy who can make containers disappear and reappear," Danny said. "The kind of guy who doesn't report to the cartel, if that's a concern."

"The fewer people who know our business, the better."

"Good, that's the way we like to do business, too," Danny said. "One thing. We don't move people or dope, so if that's what's in your container—no disrespect—we'll have to take a pass."

"We only move objects," Nadia replied.

"Excellent."

"So do you have work for us?" Genie asked.

"We have to think it over," Zander said. "We'll get back to you."

"The email we gave you is good for the rest of the week," Genie replied. She touched Danny on the back of his hand. They slid out of the booth and made their way back through the restaurant. They were on the street outside before either of them spoke.

"Think they'll bite?" Genie asked.

"They'll give us a try," Danny said. "They have to if they don't want to cut the cartel in on their side projects." He pressed the button on the car fob to unlock their Cadillac.

Genie opened the passenger's door. "It's a beautiful ploy."

Danny climbed into the driver's seat. "We were just plain lucky finding those crooked union guys. And not having to have cover jobs is a bonus."

"We've got to move fast. We've only got ten weeks to be ready for the cartel's diamond shipment."

"We'll be ready."

"You still going to take on the sister?"

Danny backed out of the parking space. "We're already in love."

BACK IN THE Blue Rose Bar and Grill, Zander switched to the other side of the booth before the server brought their lunch plates. He sipped his coffee. "What do you think, Nadia?"

Nadia set her fork down on the edge of her salad plate. "They are what we expected. Professionals. Hard to read. By reputation, they can get things done. I was surprised by how pretty she is."

"Makes her dangerous."

"I wish Johnny hadn't moved away. He was a safe, reliable guy. Always on time. Didn't ask questions."

"But he's gone," Zander said. "And our business model only works if we can transfer the occasional container out of the port without paying the cartel's thirty percent. Unless you want to start brokering the contents."

"No way. That would involve too many people. Taking an order, acting as the middleman, that's what we're good at. As long as we don't do it too often, we stay off the cartel's and the port authority's radar." She sighed. "If we didn't have to work around the cartel, life would be perfect. I wish we'd never gone in with them."

"At the time, we needed their protection. There was nothing we could do," Zander replied.

"So when do you want to try Danny and Genie?"

"Our next shipment is Ramon's cigarettes."

"The Marlboros from Pakistan?"

"It'll make a good test. Danny and Genie will take it from their port guy and bring it to us. If they get caught, you know how Ramon is, he'll cover the loss as long as he knows we did our part. And if Danny and Genie make it out to us with no problems, Ramon's guy will be there to drive it away."

"Okay," Nadia said. "Let's do it."

"I'll get in touch with Danny in a couple of days. Don't want to seem too needy, and we need to know if they can work fast."

. . .

HALFWAY ACROSS THE COUNTRY, Bruce MacBurn, Ray Johnston, and Joe Lang, Fatherland Volk white nationalists, sat at a card table with built-in chip holders in the basement family room of MacBurn's ranch-style house on a quiet cul-de-sac in Summerville, Iowa. MacBurn's wife was out with her girlfriends, which made his house the perfect place to meet. Tacked on the wall nearby was a US road map with three cities circled in red—Denver, Colorado; Independence, Missouri; and Montgomery, Ohio.

Lang, a burly, sunburned man with a tiny ponytail, studied the map. "All three?"

MacBurn, bald head covered by a ball cap, sat back and put his hand in the pockets of his blue sports coat. "Yeah, all at the same time."

"It's no problem," Johnston said. He was a tall man with a trimmed mustache and the bearing of a professional soldier. "Just set the timer and walk away. Can't be in an underground parking deck, though, 'cause it'll suppress the blast."

"Okay," Lang said, nodding, "But I still don't know why we have to deal with those sand niggers."

"Because they can get us the uranium," MacBurn said. "After we take our country back, we'll deal with their kind, scrape them right off this world just like shit off the sole of a shoe."

Johnston laughed. "Now you're talking."

"Besides," MacBurn continued, "uranium that's been processed is all marked. It's trackable to where it came from. The feds will blame the camel jockeys, and we'll be able to recruit more people to our side. It's a win-win for us."

"So the Denver mint, The Truman Presidential Library, and Wright-Patterson Air Force Base," Lang said.

"A swath straight through the middle of the country. Ought to scare the hell out of our kind of people," MacBurn replied.

"The air base and the mint I understand," Lang continued. "But why the library?"

"You ask a lot of questions," Johnston said.

"Relax, Ray. Joe's one of us."

"I just don't like too much talk."

"Just curious," Lang said.

"No problem," MacBurn continued. "We're bombing the library because that nigger- lover Truman integrated the military. That was the first step to integrated everything."

Johnston nodded. "You got that right."

"So we're all on the same page?" MacBurn asked.

"You know I'm in," Lang said. "The farm's all set. Got new locks on the barn."

"Absolutely," Johnston added.

"Okay. I'll set up a meet with the jihadi fella."

As Lang walked across MacBurn's front lawn to his car parked in the street, he turned off the digital recorder in his pants pocket. Most of a year infiltrated with these knuckleheads, and they were finally going to do something actionable. He'd begun to think he was wasting his time. He lowered the driver's side window and waved at MacBurn and Johnston as he drove away. Even though there was still plenty of summer left, the nights were cooling off, and the fresh air felt good on his face.

When he got back to the farm, he parked in the gravel in front of the one-story farmhouse and looked across the private access road to the red painted barn. Hard to believe that was where it was all going to happen. He hadn't even had to suggest it. MacBurn had come up with the idea. He locked the front door of the farmhouse behind him and went to the kitchen for a beer before he sat down at his desk in the corner of his bedroom and woke up his computer. Then he took a swig of beer, plugged the digital recorder into the computer, and clicked it on. He drank his beer, savoring every swallow, while he listened to the recording. It just got better and better. For a long time, he hadn't thought these guys were going to do anything but buy guns and talk. But here they were, finally, planning the type of terrorist act that would take them off the streets for a long time to come. He had to make sure he was at the meeting with the jihadis. When the recording finished playing, he input his password and uploaded a copy to the FBI Counterterrorism Task Force server. Special Agent-in-

Charge Jerome Victor was going to want to listen to this first thing in the morning.

TWO DAYS LATER, in Point Jericho, Danny stood in the shade by the closed boat rental kiosk on Prescott Beach. The sun was low against the cityscape to the west, and the ocean and the sky were blending into gray in the east. The freshening breeze felt good in the heat. His hands were in his sports coat pockets, his right hand around the butt of a .38 revolver. A woman in running togs ran by on the hard pack of the damp sand just above the tide, a German shepherd on a long lead racing in front of her. Danny positioned himself to look as if he were watching the sea while he kept an eye on the parking lot.

A Jeep Cherokee pulled into the lot with its headlights on and parked by itself away from the beach. Zander Hashemi, dressed in running clothes, got out and started down the path to the boat rental.

"I was beginning to think you changed your mind," Danny said.

"My daughter was late at soccer. If I set a meet, I'll be there."

"So what's the deal?"

Zander took a piece of paper out of his pocket. "Here's the specs. The ship, the container number, the GPS tracker info. It'll dock the day after tomorrow. Not sure of the time."

"And it's as we agreed?"

"Yes."

Danny read the paper. "If you want the whole container, it'll cost ten grand."

"Seven on this one. If it works out, ten on the next one."

"Will there be a next one?"

"If this one works out."

"Okay, seven it is."

"We'll look for you at the warehouse."

Zander jogged away, moving faster as he approached the hard-packed sand. Danny watched him disappear into the deepening gloom. He took out his phone as he walked back to his Cadillac. "Genie? We're on. You can work your boy."

. . .

GENIE PULLED into the gravel parking lot of the Bayside Lounge, noted Charlie Stowe's truck parked up near the door, and drove around the side of the building into an alley where she could park in the dark. She was wearing a short, tight dress with a blue-jean jacket and cowgirl boots. Plastic cups and cigarette butts littered the area in front of the door. Inside, the jukebox played Country classics, and the place was busy for a Tuesday night. She spotted Charlie at the bar, put on her game face, and sashayed over. He was a forty-something union rep with the longshoremen's union, grizzled and bored, the kind of guy who really didn't have to be convinced.

She slipped up beside him and kissed his cheek. "Hey, baby."

"Genie." He gave her a squeeze. "What's up?"

"Just another day in paradise."

"What you drinking?"

"Gin and tonic."

He nodded to the bartender, who started mixing the drink.

"Hey, Chris," Genie said.

"Hey, beautiful," the bartender replied. He set the gin and tonic in front of her.

She climbed up on a barstool. "Are you ready to do that thing?"

"When?"

"Day after tomorrow."

He drank from his beer bottle. "This Thursday?"

She nodded.

"This isn't some crazy deal?"

She rolled her eyes. "Come on. You think I want to get caught up in something stupid? This is about making a little side cash, not going to prison."

"And I make two thousand dollars?"

"You drive it out, deliver it to a friend of mine, you don't even meet the other players, you're in the clear."

"When do I get paid?"

"I bring you the cash money right after."

He took another drink.

She leaned in close and put her hand on his crotch. "Then we do some serious partying," she whispered.

"You're insane." He kissed her.

"But that's the way you like it, isn't it?"

"When can you get me the details?"

"Tomorrow."

"Okay. I can't promise I'll keep doing it, but I'll do this one." He pushed his beer bottle away. "I've got to go."

"You got time for a quickie out in the car?"

ON THURSDAY AFTERNOON, Omar Khan drove down a two-lane road through wheat fields just north of the US border. As he pulled up to a paved crossroad, he glanced at his GPS map and then down the gravel road going due south. The farmhouse must be up ahead under the distant cluster of trees. He'd flown into Winnipeg the day before and had stopped to eat lunch in Crystal City, Manitoba. He was wearing khaki pants and a blue oxford shirt, and his beard was newly trimmed, but he still stood out in the diner among all the all-so-white locals. At least he spoke English without an accent, that midwestern voice that caused no comment throughout the middle of the continent. That generally reassured the suspicious, small-town folks.

The farmhouse was in casual disrepair, a rental off the beaten track that the owners leased cheap to keep meth heads from breaking in and setting up a lab. Canola was flowering in the east field behind the house. Khan unlocked the padlock on the barn door and drove his rental car inside. The barn was empty except for a riding mower and an ATV. He transferred his roller bag to the ATV, checked the extra gas can in the back, and then rode the ATV out of the barn. A few miles to the south, he'd cross into the US.

As he drove down the dirt track to the border, he came to the section in the farm fence where the barbed wire had been cut and pulled back out of the way. He was in the right place. He pulled to a stop in the windbreak, took out his binoculars, and scanned the twenty-foot-wide, clear-cut, so-called "no touching zone" between the US and Canada. Everything was as reported. No cameras, no motion detectors, no border patrol. No drones in sight. He looked across the distance and saw a glint in the wheat field on the US side. Then a man stood and waved one hand. Khan smiled. That would be Ibrahim. Khan continued across the twenty-foot clear-cut and into the field on the other side.

Ibrahim, a blue-eyed Bosnian, smiled. "Welcome to America. God be praised."

"Yes, indeed," Khan replied, "God be praised. Is everything on track?"

Ibrahim nodded. "We're meeting the Fatherland Volk at a Holiday Inn Express near Fargo on Saturday. We have a safe house a few miles from here. You can rest, have something to eat before we get going." He climbed onto the ATV. "My motorcycle is parked by the road."

BACK IN POINT JERICHO, at 4:00 p.m., Danny sat in a stolen pickup truck outside the chain-link fence of a boarded-up warehouse in the old industrial strip by the interstate. An appliance recycler and yard waste site sat on either side, but they were both shut down for the day. A semitruck pulled up. Charlie Stowe, wearing blue coveralls and a ballcap, climbed out of the cab.

"You sure this is the one?" Danny asked.

"Yep."

"You disable the GPS?"

"This isn't the first container I've lifted."

"Take the pickup. Drop it in a public place. And keep your gloves on."

"What about my money?"

"Genie will bring it."

Danny drove the semitruck onto the freeway, got off two exits down, turned around and drove back to town. No one was tailing him. A light rain started to fall. He got off on Chance Martin Drive, continued into the warehouse district near the port, turned onto Blue

Gill Way, pulled in behind the Hashemi Carpets & Arts building, and backed up to the loading dock.

He was waiting at the loading dock when Zander came out the back door of the warehouse holding an umbrella. "Is this the one?"

"That's what the man said," Danny replied. "But let's have a look." He opened the container doors. Boxes were stacked to the ceiling. Zander pulled one box out onto the loading dock and cut the top open. It was full of cartons of Marlboro cigarettes. He smiled. "Let me get your money."

He disappeared into the warehouse and came back in a minute with an accordion envelope. "Seven thousand dollars, as we agreed."

Danny put the envelope inside his jacket.

"Aren't you going to count it?"

"Zander, you're a businessman, and you know who I am, so I know the money is right. Keep us in mind."

"I will."

As Zander put the open box back into the container and shut the doors, Danny climbed down from the loading dock and crossed the parking lot to his Cadillac. A man dressed in jeans and a cowboy hat came out of the warehouse and climbed into the cab of the semi-truck. Danny watched the semitruck drive away. A well-oiled machine. The truck was here and gone, lickity-split. There was nothing to connect the truck or the cargo to the Hashemis. He and Genie had cleared five thousand on this little job and were on their way to earning Zander's trust. He put his car in drive.

AN HOUR AND A HALF LATER, Charlie Stowe was sitting at the bar in the Bayside Lounge when Genie came through the door. "I Never Promised You A Rose Garden" was blaring from the jukebox. Happy hour was winding down, but the place was still half full of men who didn't want to go home.

"Hey, sugar." She sidled up to him, kissed his cheek, and placed an envelope in his lap.

He squeezed it, but he didn't open it.

"I told you this was easy money," she whispered. She looked up at the bartender. "Hey, Chris, you got a gin and tonic for me?"

"Coming at you."

She turned back to Stowe. "There wasn't any trouble on your end, was there?"

"No, it's no problem as long as it's not too often. Port police see a pattern, then you're screwed."

"Then we're just going to make sure that doesn't happen." She ran her hand up and down Stowe's back. Chris slid her drink in front of her. Stowe's phone rang. He looked at the screen. "I have to take this."

He walked out into the parking lot before he answered the call. A man who was driving away waved to him. He spoke into his phone. "Hey, honey."

"Where are you?"

"I got tied up with some union business."

"Your dinner is cold."

"Lost track of time."

"You were supposed to pick up Stephanie from cheer-team practice."

"Christ. You're right. I'm leaving now."

"Too late. She caught a ride with Bobbie. Besides, I don't want her riding with you when you're drunk."

"I'm not drunk."

"You're always drunk when you come home from union business."

"Penny—"

"Your plate will be in the refrigerator." She hung up.

He looked at the screen on his phone. All he saw was the reflection of the lights from the Bayside Lounge. "Damn it," he muttered.

He bumped into a table as he walked back through the bar.

"Everything okay?" Genie asked.

"Yeah, everything's fine." He took a swig from his beer bottle. "You want to do some real partying?"

"I'm all yours, baby."

"Let's get a motel room. Stop by the package store for a bottle."

"Leave my car here?"

"I'll bring you back."

THEY DROVE AWAY from the bar, neither saying a word, Genie feeling Stowe's conflict and thinking it was best not to get in the middle of what was on his mind. Stowe pulled up in front of Lightning Liquors. The parking lot was empty. "Vodka and Coke?"

She nodded. "Whatever you want, sugar. I'll wait here."

He trudged up to the door. She could hear the bell ring above the door as he pulled it open. She got out her phone. "It's me."

"I was beginning to worry," Danny said.

"I'll be late. I think he got a call from his wife. Or maybe another girlfriend. He wants to spend some time."

"Do I need to come over there to keep an eye on you?"

"Please. He's wrapped around my finger. I'll be hearing his confession before we're through."

"Love you."

"Love you, too."

2

WORKING THE PLAN

The next morning, Danny slipped out of bed early, taking care not to wake Genie, got dressed, and drove downtown. He knew that Nadia always went to Rudy's Coffee and Books first thing in the morning to have her coffee and read the newspaper. And there she was, at a table in the window in the photography section, dressed for her day, modest, dark-colored outfit, her hair pulled back at the nape of her neck, a large ceramic cup on the table in front of her.

He came through the door, headed to the coffee counter, put in his order, turned to the room, and put on a bemused smile, as if he'd just noticed her. He headed for her table. "Mind if I join you?"

Nadia looked up from her newspaper. "Danny. Yeah, sure, sit down."

"This is a great little bookstore."

"I like it," she replied. "They have great coffee, too." She set her newspaper to one side. "Have you been here before?"

"A few times, not this early, though."

The tattooed man behind the counter called his name. "Excuse me." He got his coffee and came back to the table. "Is this your morning place?"

"Yeah, I always get my coffee here. It's peaceful in the morning. Only a few people and no one I know. I like a little quiet time before I go in to the office."

"The office." He sipped his coffee. "Looks like our little arrangement is going to work out."

"That's what Zander says."

"Hope we get some more action soon."

"It's not up to me."

"You and your brother—how long have you been in the import business?"

"Our father started it after he emigrated. Our uncle is still in Iran. He handles that end. Of course, it's all gotten complicated since the embargo."

"And then your father retired?"

"Our father and mother are both gone."

"Sorry to hear that."

"What about you?"

"I'm an orphan. And, you know, I do a little of this and that."

She smiled. "Just a straight-up hustler?"

"Yeah. We just try to find ways to add value."

"What about your wife? Where did you meet?"

"Genie? She's not my wife. She's my business partner."

"But the wedding rings."

"In our line of work, it just makes things easier. Regular guys won't bother her, and philanderers—well, they can often be useful."

"How so?"

"A person who wants what they're not supposed to have can often be persuaded to do things we need done."

"Sounds dangerous."

He shrugged. "Like most things, Nadia, it's only dangerous if you don't know what you're doing." He glanced at his watch. "Wow. I've got to go. Good talking to you. Maybe I'll see you again."

"Maybe."

.   .   .

LATER THAT MORNING, Zander came into Nadia's office while she was at her computer, going over the monthly financial report. "Have you got the invoices on the last shipment from India? That new vendor. Have those been filed yet?"

"What's up?"

"I think there may be a size discrepancy with some of the rugs. I want to crosscheck with the invoices."

"The paper ones?"

"Yeah."

Nadia pushed back her chair, wheeled around to a two-drawer file cabinet, and pulled out a file folder. "Here you go."

"Great. Thanks." He opened the file folder and started poking through the invoices.

She turned back to her computer. "I saw Danny this morning."

Zander closed the file folder. "Where?"

"Rudy's."

"What did he want?"

"He was making conversation. Said he and Genie are just business partners."

"Did he say anything you believed?"

"I don't know."

"But you like him?"

"I do. I don't have to pretend around him."

"You know he can't be trusted—not him or the woman."

"I know."

"We've got everything at stake."

"I know."

"My family, my daughter, the sacrifices your husband Pauly made to ensure our safety."

"I'm not a little girl, Zander, and you don't have to be my big brother all the time."

"I'm not saying you don't know what you're doing. I'm just saying we've got to be careful."

"Apology accepted."

Zander shook his head. "I'm going back to the warehouse."

. . .

ON SATURDAY EVENING, at the Holiday Inn Express on a freeway inter-change just outside Fargo, North Dakota, Khan and Ibrahim walked down the second-floor hallway, their hands on the butts of the pistols in their jacket pockets. "Room 247?" Ibrahim asked.

"Yes," Khan replied. "We're looking for a bald man named MacBurn."

They stopped in front of the room. Ibrahim knocked. The door opened. MacBurn, a ball cap on his head, stood in the doorway. "Khan?"

"Yes."

"I didn't know there would be another fella."

"No one can do anything alone."

"Come on in."

Khan and Ibrahim stepped into the room and stood with their hands in their pockets and their backs to the closed door. "I see you also have friends," Khan said.

"Lang and Johnston," MacBurn said. "Just in case I can't make a meeting."

Khan nodded toward his companion. "Ibrahim."

"Let's get on with this," Lang said. "None of us want to be here too long."

"Relax, Lang," MacBurn said. "No one knows we're here."

"But your friend is right," Khan said. "Let's get down to business. I have to admit we were surprised when you reached out to us."

"We have some shared interests," MacBurn said.

"Such as?"

"You want the US out of your business, and we want our govern-ment to start focusing on home. Everyone who doesn't belong here needs to go back where they belong."

Khan smiled. "Everyone should keep to themselves. Mind their own business."

"Exactly."

"How can we help you?"

"We need some uranium."

"What for?"

"You know what for."

"For a dirty bomb? Why not find some here?"

"'Cause the government can tell where it came from. It needs to come from overseas."

"So they will blame us?"

"Is that a problem? I thought you jihadis would want the credit."

"Uranium is a big ask. Do you know how to do the rest of it?"

"Johnston knows how. He's army taught."

Khan paused, looking from MacBurn to Johnston to Lang and back again. "This is not an easy thing. As soon as we know when and where, we will be in touch. Anything else?"

MacBurn shook his head.

"Give us a thirty-minute head start."

Khan and Ibrahim took the stairs at the end of the hall down to the lobby. A bored young woman stood behind the reception counter watching the Weather Channel on the TV mounted to the ceiling. She barely glanced toward them as they left through the front doors into the parking lot. The night air was cool. The lot was full of pickup trucks and SUVs. They got in their rental Nissan Sentra and headed for the freeway on ramp.

"Will we actually help them?" Ibrahim asked. "Can we be sure they are who they claim to be?"

"I would not have come if there were any doubt."

"But they hate us."

"Yes, but they hate their own government more, so we will use them. These are simple-minded men. They watch too many spy movies. Seriously radioactive material is too hard to transport unde-tected. We have tried several times. The containers to shield the uranium are too large and heavy. But something more low level, something that would get them to plant the bombs for us, we could make that happen."

"Bring it in through Canada?"

"No, the Canadian route is too valuable. We'll have someone else bring it in. That way if there is a problem, it won't fall on us."

BACK IN THE MOTEL ROOM, Lang pushed aside the curtain and looked out the window into the parking lot, where two FBI field agents were working their way through the parked cars.

"What you looking at, Joe?" Johnston asked. "No one followed us here."

"You sure about that? You sure someone's not following the jihadis?"

"We'll take the end door down the stairs that leads out to the pool. That's why we parked on that side. No one will see our faces."

"We've waited long enough," MacBurn said. "We've got a lot of driving ahead of us."

"You two go on down. I want to wipe the room for fingerprints," Lang said.

Johnston sighed. "There's no need to. The maids will clear it up."

"Just want to be sure."

"Suit yourself," MacBurn said. "Just hurry it up."

MacBurn and Johnston left the room. Lang pulled the TV out, reached in back of it, and pulled out the surveillance hard drive he'd hidden there. He put the drive in his jacket pocket. Then he lifted Johnston's fingerprints off the TV remote control and MacBurn's off the toilet handle. He put the fingerprint cards in his wallet. Too bad the jihadis hadn't touched anything. That would have been a real bonus. He looked at the text messages on his phone. A field agent had planted a tracking device on the jihadis' car. He erased the message. Did he have time for a quick call? He speed-dialed Special Agent-in-Charge Victor.

"The terrorists have agreed to supply the uranium."

"Your playmates are some bad players for sure, but the court is not going to just accept your testimony. We need hard evidence, or they'll just say we entrapped some goofballs. So you've got to stay with them. No leadership from you. They have to take all the steps on their own. You're just there to document and collect evidence."

"Yes, sir."

"Did you tag the terrorists?"

"Nelson and Boyd are on them."

"Good work. We'll deal with them. You stay focused on the Fatherland Volk connection."

ON MONDAY, Nadia was having a late lunch with her friend Julie at The Clam Chowder, a casual restaurant in the downtown shopping district where they liked the daily soup and salad combo. They had been in and out of two dress shops and three shoe stores, window shopping mainly, although Julie had bought a sweater, and Nadia had bought a pair of sparkly black flats. They were planning the rest of the afternoon's shopping when Danny walked up to their table.

"Wow," he said. "It's like we're following each other around."

"You come here often?" Nadia replied.

"This is my lunch spot, but I prefer the sandwiches to the soups."

Julie studied his face. "I don't think we've met."

"Danny Briggs. I'm new in town. But I like this place, so maybe we'll meet again." He turned to Nadia. "I don't want to interrupt your lunch. Just wanted to say hi." He squeezed her hand. Then he turned back to Julie. "Good to meet you."

Julie waited for Danny to walk out the door before she spoke. "Okay, Nadia, spill. Who is that guy?"

"He's a client."

"A client? He held your hand. He was almost flirting with you."

"You're imagining things."

"Yeah, I'm imagining things all right. For a minute there I thought he was going to lean down and kiss you."

"Stop it."

"You're blushing."

"Really, Julie, that's enough."

"You've got nothing to be ashamed of. You're single. You haven't been on a date in forever."

"I know. I know. I just don't know if I'm ready, and I don't know if

I'd date that guy even if I was ready."

"Why not? He's good-looking. Obviously interested in you. It's just a date. I could call you in the middle in case you wanted to escape."

"Enough about that."

"Okay. I'm just saying it's never the perfect time."

NADIA STOPPED BACK by the office in the late afternoon just to take a look through her emails. Nothing that couldn't wait until tomorrow. She found her brother in the warehouse, down on his knees examining one of the Indian rugs he was concerned about. He saw her come through from the office. "How was Julie?"

"As exuberant as always."

"And the shopping?"

She waved a hand dismissively. "A waste, really. But I did find a fun pair of shoes. What's the verdict here?"

"Three of the rugs are undersized. But, come look here. The colors, the density, the feel, all superb. So we'll make our money. Just have to be careful with this producer."

"Better tell Uncle."

"I will."

"I ran into Danny again."

Zander stood up. "Where this time?"

"At The Clam Chowder. Julie and I were having lunch."

"That was no accident."

"I know."

"He's up to something."

"Maybe it's not business."

"So he was flirting with you?"

"I don't know. That's what Julie thinks."

"People in his line of work—they're only loyal to themselves. They're always angling because they have nothing to tie them down."

"Once upon a time, that was Pauly."

"You're right."

"And you didn't like him, either."

"Until Pauly proved he was one of us."

"And maybe Danny is going to prove himself. Look, I'm not saying I'd go out with him. Or that anything is going to happen."

"I know. And maybe Genie isn't his woman, and maybe everything will turn out fine." He shook his head. "I know you're lonely, Sis. But this guy? You could do better."

She walked out into the parking lot. The sun was already behind the nearby buildings. Typical Zander, always overprotective, but he was right about one thing. She was lonely. But was Julie right? Was she holding herself back, expecting to know too much before she would even take a chance? Going on a date, having some fun—what could be wrong with that? But if it became the serious relationship she wanted, what would she do then? Would she have to start keeping secrets, just like Zander did from Bonnie? With Pauly, it had never been an issue. He'd known everything. And now he was dead. Was that her choice? To keep secrets or to be with a man who was always at risk? Was that what was holding her back?

LATER, after dark, Genie and Stowe were in the back seat of her car on a service road on the far side of the city park. They were still lying together after sex, their breathing coming back down, the last of the rush ebbing away. Genie sat up, hooked her bra, and pulled her sweater down. She found her pants and underwear on the floorboard. Stowe pulled his pants and underwear up all at one time, and then shifted his legs around to the floor. His phone was buzzing in his pocket.

"I've got to quit doing this. My wife is catching on."

"Then we've just got to be more careful. We've got a good thing going on here, don't we? You, me, fun times, no strings. You are having fun, aren't you?"

He smiled. "No complaints."

"And, as a bonus, we're making some side money. We keep our heads down, sugar, don't get greedy, we can milk this money train."

"Okay, but we've got to cool it for now. We can't take a container every week if we don't want to get caught."

She kissed him. "Want to catch a few drinks?"

"I've got to go home."

"Okay." They got out of the back seat and into the front. She drove back down the service road toward the park entrance, taking care to avoid the potholes.

"You should take your wife on a real date. Get dressed up. Buy her flowers. Take her to a fancy restaurant. Tell her it's to make up for being an asshole."

"An asshole?"

"You know what I mean—an idiot who hasn't been paying attention, who forgot what was important. You want her happy, don't you?"

"Yeah, I do."

Genie took a right onto Clayman Road. "Then, after the date, when you get home, tell her how important she is to you, how much you love her. Write it up and memorize it ahead of time. You can't sell it if there's too many *uhs* in it."

"She won't believe me."

"Are you kidding? She'll suck it up. She hasn't left you, has she? That means she still wants to believe."

"You've done this before."

"Been married twice. Should have listened to my own advice."

ON A WINDY WEDNESDAY afternoon in Moline, Illinois, Johnston and Lang walked down the aisle of Deep Discount Used Cars. Up ahead, they saw exactly what they were looking for, a 2007 Chevrolet Express Cargo Van. It was white, with rust showing at the edges of the doors. "What do you think?" Lang asked.

"It's the V8," Johnston replied. He opened the driver's door to look at the dashboard. "It's got 148,231 miles. That's a little high."

A salesman walked up to them, his hands in the pockets of his jacket. "Hey, guys. Looking for a work van? This one has still got a lot of life."

"What do you want for it?" Lang asked.

"This van will hold a lot of gear, and it won't let you down. It's got a clean maintenance record. Take it for a drive. You'll see it's the real deal."

Johnston nodded. "I hear you, but what's the price?"

The salesman shuffled from one foot to the other. "It's $7,200, title, registration, the works."

Johnston opened Kelley Blue Book on his phone. "I'll give you $5,500 if it checks out on the drive and the maintenance record is good."

"The maintenance record will check out, and you're going to love the way it handles, but I can't go that low."

"Then we could split the difference. How about $6,350? That would be our highest offer."

"Let me talk to my manager. Then we'll take it for a drive while he thinks it over. Be right back."

"Hey, $6,350 is a good price," Lang said.

"I think I could have pushed him a little lower, but I didn't want him remembering us." Johnston walked around the van, examining the tires and opening the other doors. "Since you're going to be driving it, you want to do the test drive?"

"Sure."

"Here he comes. Let's get this done and get out of here."

BACK IN POINT JERICHO, Danny and Genie lay tangled together in the sheets of their bed in their two-bedroom rental house on Jefferson Street. Their house was one among a buffer of rentals that separated the home owners from the apartments next to the freeway. Danny kissed her and rolled onto his back. "I've been missing you."

"And I've missed you," she replied. "Stowe thinks two minutes is a half hour."

"But he's still on the hook?"

"Yeah, he's getting a little skittish, so I did the marital advice routine, told him I'd been divorced twice."

"That bit never gets old, does it?"

"No, it doesn't."

Danny turned his head to look at Genie's profile. "I think Nadia's ready."

She kept looking at the ceiling. "You haven't slept with her yet."

"This just has a different rhythm than usual. I'm going to sweep her off her feet."

She turned to find his eyes. "You're going full romance?"

"She's not going to sell out her brother. She doesn't just screw around, and her husband was in the game, so romance is the best way in."

"It's your call. You want to practice some of that tenderness?"

"You are the devil."

"Just wanting to help. Happy to hear some sweetness."

"I've got something else in mind for you, but it's going to have to wait."

"Promises, promises."

Danny picked up his phone from the bedside table and input Billy's number.

"Mister, what can I do for you?"

"I need a computer guy."

"Have to be a guy? What about a gal?"

"It's a straight-up tech job. I just need the best."

"I'll look into it. Someone will be in touch in the next few hours."

Danny set his phone down on his chest. "You want to go to dinner, or do you want to get some delivery?"

"Let's go out. There's that Thai place downtown."

"Over by the Blue Rose?"

"I think it's a block down."

The Thai restaurant was busy with no one who knew them. The food was good, not too spicy, and the background noise was just loud enough for a private conversation. Danny's phone rang. "Yeah?"

"Traveling Man? It's Becky."

"Becky, good to hear from you. How are the kids?"

"Off at school. What's the job?"

"I need you to clone a phone and use it to hack into an office Wi-

Fi and access a computer."

"Not a problem. When do you need it?"

"Next week. You'll probably be here a few days while we set the opportunity."

"What's the pay?"

"This is a salary job. You'll be in and out, so you'll collect your usual fee."

"Can you cover the travel?"

"For you, Becky? Yeah. I'll let Billy know."

"I'll be waiting for your call."

He put his phone away.

"So Billy reached out to Becky?" Genie asked.

Danny nodded.

"She's our kind of people."

"Yeah, she's good at her job and won't cheat a partner." He glanced around for their server. "You ready for the check?"

Two DAYS LATER, Genie was warming a barstool in the Bayside Lounge, the ice from a gin and tonic in the glass in front of her, waiting for Stowe to come in. She wanted to hear about how his campaign with his wife was going, give him some reinforcement, keep him close for when they needed him. A bearlike man, loose suit and an acne-scarred face, sat down at the end of the bar. He was watching her while he was pretending not to watch her. She picked up her glass and pretended to drink. She was glad of the Glock in her shoulder bag.

Stowe came in, waved toward a few friends, and sat down beside her. The bartender put a bottle of beer in front of him before he could ask. Stowe took a long pull from the bottle and set it down with a sigh.

"Hard day at work?"

"Work is my vacation. I've got a hard day at home."

"Why's that?"

"Sucking up to the wife is a full-time job."

"She must be very happy."

"She's orgasmically happy. She's got this goofy grin on her face, and she's got all day to make plans for the two of us after I come home. She's killing me."

"But you're not in the dog house anymore, are you?"

"Thanks a lot."

The bearlike man shuffled down the bar and sat on the other side of Stowe. "Charlie," he said. "How you doing?"

"Getting by."

He glanced at Genie. "We thought you were just dipping your wick with this cutie pie, but now we've found out that you pulled a job at the port."

"Hey, Jimbo—"

"Don't try to deny it; we don't care, okay? So long as you don't interfere with our plans. But from here on out, you're going to keep me informed, and you're going to pay your tax. Nothing happens at the port that we don't get a part of."

Stowe hung his head. "Okay."

Jimbo patted Stowe's cheek. "That's a good boy." He ambled out of the bar. The other customers tried not to see him.

Stowe drained his beer. "You heard him."

"But he didn't say no, and he didn't say we had to pay the back taxes."

"You aren't kidding, are you?"

"It's still good money, even if we have to give him a share. We just have to be more careful about which shipments we take."

"I don't know."

"Relax, Charlie. Let's have another drink, unwind, get a little perspective."

"I can't stay. I've got to get home. Keep the wife happy."

"I'm proud of you, Charlie. You've really turned your wife around." She rubbed her hand up and down his thigh. "But have you got enough time for me to rock your world?"

"I've got to go."

"You sure you don't have time for a quickie?"

"A quickie?"

"I'm parked around back."

AFTERWARD, Genie drove back to their rental house and parked in the driveway behind Danny's Cadillac.

"There you are," he said. "Got some Mexican takeout. It's still hot."

"I need to shower first. I've got Charlie Stowe all over me." She kicked off her shoes.

"Is there a problem?"

"Cartel guy is onto our scam. We have to tell them when we're going to lift a container, and we have to pay the tax."

"So Stowe balked?"

"Yeah, I had to cool him out."

"But it worked?"

"I think so. Just need to keep him close. If he starts thinking for himself, it could be a problem." She unzipped her skirt and stepped out of it.

"But you've set the hooks tight. He thinks about his extra money, he thinks about you. He thinks about things going better with his wife, he thinks about you."

She started unbuttoning her blouse. "I'm just saying I need to keep an eye on him."

"I got you. Take your shower. I'll keep the food warm. You want beer or wine with dinner?"

"Beer."

EVEN THOUGH IT WAS A BEAUTIFUL, sunny afternoon in Dublin, Ireland, Major Javad Tehrani of the Iranian Revolutionary Guard walked past the outdoor seating at Milani's Pastries and found a seat at a small table crowded into the back corner. He was dressed like a tourist. He took a guidebook from his jacket pocket and thumbed through it while he waited for the server. When she came to his table he ordered coffee. A few minutes later, Omar Khan came through the door. He was clean-shaven and carried a small backpack on one shoulder. He spotted Tehrani and joined him. They spoke in English.

"Good to see you, old friend," Khan said. "How was your trip?"

"Uneventful, though I must admit I was surprised to receive your message," Tehrani replied.

"Some things are better not written down."

"But it is difficult for me to travel without raising suspicion."

"And yet here you are."

The server brought Tehrani's coffee. "Nothing for me," Khan said. Tehrani looked at Khan expectantly.

Khan lowered his voice. "We need your help transporting some depleted uranium into the US."

"My superiors won't like that."

"That hasn't stopped you before."

"Moving artifacts is innocent enough."

"And you were well paid."

Tehrani stirred his coffee. "Where does this uranium come from?"

"Some brothers in Iraq. Don't worry, it can't be tied to your country. On the contrary, we don't want to share the credit."

"This sounds like something I don't want to be part of."

Khan shook his head. "Thus far, you've been a dabbler. You've taken our money, and you've taken no risk. Now it's your time to serve the great Jihad. Unless you want your government to find out what you've been doing."

"You'd really turn on me?"

"We're all just pieces on the board, Tehrani, all of us. We either serve God or we are swept away."

"If you do this, this smuggling route will probably be compromised. It will be of no use in the future, and our people in America will be found out."

"There will always be another smuggling route."

"So you've made up your mind?"

"Yes. My people will be in contact the usual way."

"How soon?"

"Very soon, my friend." Khan stood up. "It is good to see you. Enjoy your vacation."

Tehrani watched Khan walk away. What a smug bastard. Depleted uranium. This was troubling. What could One World Jihad Union possibly be planning? Exploding a dirty bomb inside the United States was a fool's errand. Anyone even remotely connected would be hounded to the ends of the earth. If his superiors found out he was even the least bit involved, he'd be shot in prison.

He kept watch on who was coming and going through the front door of the pastry shop. Khan had him in a tight place, that was certain. He'd been a fool to take his money. But it was too late to back out now. And the Hashemis had a perfect record moving contraband through the port of Point Jericho. Why should this particular package be any different? He finished his coffee and set some money on the table. His wife and his family were depending on him. All he could do now was make sure this job came off without a hitch.

On Tuesday, back in Point Jericho, Becky Gable, a thin black woman with short, natural hair, stood under the awning in front of the airport baggage claim waiting for her ride. She pulled up the collar of her raincoat. A soft rain was falling, and cars were jockeying for position in the street, sliding into spots to pick up passengers or pulling back out into traffic.

Genie pulled up in a Toyota and lowered the passenger window. "Hey, girl."

Becky shoved her suitcase into the back seat and climbed into the front. "Genie, it's been a long time."

"Yes, it has."

"Did you get my equipment?"

"Two packages arrived for you yesterday."

"When is the job?"

"Maybe today or tomorrow."

"Then I better get set up. Where have you got me?"

"You're staying with us."

3

NADIA

On Thursday, at the Hashemi warehouse, Zander pried the top off a packing crate that had arrived in a container with a shipment of artifacts. Inside, packed in straw, was a smaller box. He put on latex gloves before he laid the smaller box on a workbench and ran a boxcutter down the tape, taking care not to damage the box. Inside was what appeared to be a very old book. He lifted the cover gingerly. Ancient calligraphy in a language he couldn't read. Hand-colored drawings with gold embellishments in the margins. Was it a stolen antiquity or a forgery? Either way, there had been too many of these packages lately. Maybe he was just being paranoid, but he wanted to get it out of the warehouse as soon as possible, and he didn't want to be seen making another delivery.

He retaped the box, taking care to line up the new tape with the original tape, before he carried it through from the warehouse to his office. Nadia was out, but he would never put her at risk. Besides, women weren't welcome at the Oasis Café. And he couldn't take a chance on one of their employees. The less they knew about the work they did for Tehrani, the better. He set the box on his desk and sat down. A large, framed display on the far wall showed the origins of the various fibers and dyes used in their carpets. How had they gotten involved with smuggling artifacts for the jihadis? Uncle had needed to grease a palm in Iran, and cash hadn't worked. Place the artifact among the legitimate art objects, Uncle had said. The authorities will never know the difference. One time led to two times, the promise of never again, and here they were. Still, they were only moving antiquities. Nothing to keep a person from sleeping at night. They might even be saving the objects for future generations by getting them out of a war zone. But customs enforcement wouldn't see it that way. If they got caught, they would lose their business and probably go to jail.

Zander ran his hand along the top of the box, pressing down the tape. Maybe he could ask Danny. Danny would know how to make contact, how to take care, and if he were arrested, he'd keep his mouth shut. And as long as he didn't think he'd been set up, he wouldn't be seeking revenge. He didn't trust Danny, but that didn't matter. Danny had an interest in maintaining their relationship as long as he thought he might make more money moving containers from the port. And he wouldn't find out anything useful at the Oasis Café. It was worth a try. He got out his phone. "Danny?"

"Yeah."

"Could you do me a favor?"

"Depends on what it is."

"Could you deliver a package for me?"

"What kind of package?"

"Not drugs or weapons or anything like that."

"Why not deliver it yourself?"

"I've been to this place too many times recently."

"It's that kind of deal?"

"That's why I need your help."

"Okay. You at the office?"

"Yes."

"I'll stop by in an hour."

Zander ended the call. If things went badly, it would be a problem. He'd lose the artifact, and he'd need a new connection at the port, but at least he wouldn't be the one who was arrested. And if things went well—which, let's face it, was the most likely outcome—he'd owe Danny a favor. He'd need to pull him in closer, show him that he valued their relationship. Not something he looked forward to, but it couldn't be helped. He should plan on taking him out to dinner. Maybe there was still time to make a restaurant reservation.

DANNY WAS SMILING when set his phone on the kitchen table.

"What's up?" Genie asked. Becky looked up from the tablet computer she was setting up.

"Zander wants me to drop a package for him."

"He doesn't like you," Genie replied.

"He didn't lie about it. He wants to know if the drop-off is still safe."

"Doesn't mean he's not throwing you in the fire."

"There's bound to be some risk. But I'll find out something about their illegal operation, and he'll trust me just a little bit more."

"Want me to go with you?"

"No, you should stay here with Becky. Make sure you're ready to go if I call with an opportunity to clone Nadia's phone."

AFTER DANNY PICKED up the box, he drove down into a neighborhood of rundown rowhouses near the port where temporary workers and day laborers lived. On the corner of Fifth and Garfield, he found the place he was looking for—the Oasis Café, a coffee shop/deli that served the immigrant community. He pulled up to the curb. The steel gate on the front door was open, as well as the gates on the windows. Two men in worn-out work clothes sat on the steps to the right of the coffee shop entrance. Across the street, two women wearing headscarves and long dresses were stopped on the sidewalk with their baby strollers, chatting. Upstairs, above them, with a clear view of the coffee shop entrance, a geezer wearing a Muslim hat sat looking out the window. There was nothing about this picture that seemed right—not the working men, not the women, not the geezer. But they were obviously not cops.

Danny pushed through the glass door. There was a deli counter to the right and five tables to the left, all full. A chalkboard behind the counter listed the menu in English and in some Middle Eastern language. Everyone in the place turned to look at him, not even pretending to be discreet. They were all men, all with their jackets on, all with the neutral expression that said "you're not welcome here."

An unshaven man of Middle Eastern origin, wearing a white apron over a flannel shirt, stood behind the counter.

"You Jimmy?" Danny asked.

The man smiled a crooked smile, revealing a broken tooth. He spoke with an accent. "Who's asking?"

"Got a package for you." Danny set the box on the counter.

"You sure?"

"This is where I was told to leave it."

"Then leave it."

Danny got back into his car. The two men, the moms, and the geezer were all still in place. He got out his phone and called Zander. "You sure you gave me the right address?"

Zander described the corner and the coffee shop.

"Okay, then. The job's done."

"Thanks. I appreciate it. Nadia and I are having dinner at Wyatt's. Why don't you join us? You and Genie. Seven p.m."

"We'll be there."

He pulled away from the curb, drove three blocks up, circled two blocks to the left, and rolled through a yellow light to make sure he wasn't being followed. The after-work traffic was just beginning to trickle onto the streets. In twenty minutes, he was parked in the driveway of their rental house behind Genie's Toyota.

Genie and Becky were still at the kitchen table. Becky was inputting code into a laptop computer that was cabled to the tablet.

"How'd it go?" Genie asked.

He filled them in.

"So Zander is making deliveries to some sort of ethnic gang. Not something I would have expected," Genie said.

"I know. A lot more risk than you'd think he'd want to take on."

"Wonder where the packages come from?"

"Good question," Danny said.

"And we've been invited to dinner." Genie googled Wyatt's Supper Club on her phone. "They have live music tonight."

"This could be our chance to clone Nadia's phone," Danny said.

"Zander didn't waste any time showing the love, did he?"

"No, he didn't. He's just a little too obvious, but it works to our advantage." Danny turned to Becky. "You got the programming figured out?"

"You get me the phone, and I'll get you hooked up."

"Okay. Genie will take the handoff, and you'll clone the phone in her car in the parking lot. How long will it take?"

"Using my custom program, a couple of minutes."

"Then you'll bring the phone back to Genie."

"How are you going to get the phone?" Becky asked.

"We'll figure that out on the fly."

MacBurn and Lang took the exit of off Interstate 25 North onto East Eisenhower Boulevard in Loveland, Colorado. All the lanes were full, but all the cars were traveling faster than the speed limit. "Keep to the left," MacBurn said. "The Best Western is right there."

"I see it," Lang replied. He took a left at the light and rolled into the Best Western parking lot. "Thank God, we're finally here. That's a lot of driving for one day."

"It's worth it, though. If the vans are all bought near to where they're blown up, it'll make our organization seem a lot bigger. The Feds will be looking for three groups, not one."

"Glad I'm not driving to Ohio." Lang pulled into a parking spot across from the motel.

"Don't know that yet. If Ray can't get off work the same days as me, then it'll be you and one of us again."

"Not if I get that post office job."

"You really think you've got a chance?"

"I got a good score on the exam, and I've got military points."

"Are those better than minority points? You know they're going to hire every minority and woman before they even look at your application."

"Don't be dragging me down."

"I'm just saying, buddy. You know how it is."

They climbed out of their truck. "I'm starving," Lang said.

"Let's get checked in first." MacBurn led the way into the Best Western.

"Where do you want to eat?" Lang asked.

"Isn't there a Chili's around here somewhere?"

DANNY AND GENIE stood at the hostess station in Wyatt's Supper Club. He was wearing a charcoal suit with a light blue shirt, and she was wearing a deep blue dress chosen to show off her assets. Beyond the hostess station, the main room was filled with round tables covered with white tablecloths. A stage, set with a piano and music stands, occupied the back of the room next to a small dance floor. Even though it was a Thursday, the tables were full.

"Reservations?" the hostess asked.

"We're with the Hashemis."

She looked at her tablet. "Follow me."

As she led them across the room, they spotted Zander and Nadia seated at a table near to the stage. Zander stood up. "Danny, Genie, so glad you could come."

"Wouldn't miss it for the world," Danny said. He and Zander shook hands. He sat next to Nadia, Genie next to Zander. Danny continued. "We thought we might get to meet your wife."

"We couldn't get a sitter on such short notice."

Nadia cut in. "Weeknight."

"Maybe another time," Genie said.

They chitchatted through dinner. After the server collected the dishes and brought their coffee, Zander asked, "So what did you think of the Oasis Café?"

"Honestly?" Danny replied. "I don't know what you've seen, but it looked like a rough spot. The neighborhood watch wasn't working for the police, and the café itself was full of people who weren't customers. Reminded me of an old-fashioned gangsters' social club."

"Really? So I've got nothing to worry about from the police when I go down there?"

"I didn't say that."

The lights dimmed and the musicians came out on stage. "I'm going to the ladies," Nadia said. She picked up her handbag.

"Me too," Genie said. As she got up, she squeezed Danny's shoulder. He covered his mouth and coughed to indicate he understood that she was going to make a try for the phone, then pulled his own phone out onto his thigh and texted an exclamation point to Becky, who was waiting in the back hallway.

When Genie and Nadia entered the hallway to the restrooms, Genie asked, "You going to take the opportunity to look at your messages?"

"No, it's just work stuff. I'm not working tonight."

"Good for you."

Becky barreled out of the ladies room and bumped Nadia into Genie, who slipped her hand into Nadia's purse and lifted her phone. "I'm so sorry," Becky said. "I'm just such a doofus tonight. That last glass of wine must have gone to my head."

"No worries," Nadia said.

Genie slipped the phone to Becky behind her back.

Genie and Nadia continued into the restroom. "I hope she's not driving," Nadia said.

When they came out of the restroom, the band, a quintet, was working through a set of jazz standards. Several couples were on the dance floor. Before Nadia could sit down, Danny stood up. He held out his hand. "Want to dance?"

"Well, it's been a long time."

"Then now's the time to change that."

He led her to the dance floor where they crowded in, his hands clasping hers, and fell into a swing step. After they found their rhythm, he said, "Time to twirl." He let go with his left hand and lifted his right up and around. She twirled under his arm, and then he snapped her back in close. She smiled. She leaned her face toward him. "I'd forgotten how much fun this is."

Back at the table, Genie was acting as if she was immersed in the band's performance. Her phone vibrated. It was a text from Becky. Nadia's phone was cloned. She texted back an emoji thumbs up.

As the band finished the song, Danny pulled Nadia around the corner into the hallway. "What are you doing?" she asked.

"I've got something in mind."

Nadia could feel her heart pounding. She was having so much fun—more fun than she'd remembered having for a long time. She didn't want it to stop. And why should she? Julie was right. One date didn't mean anything. No matter what she did. There was nothing wrong with wanting to be touched, wanting to feel that wild happiness, if only for a few moments. No matter what happened afterward, nothing would be able to take it away. She smiled her brightest, most sincere smile. He smiled back. She kissed him. "You know my brother doesn't approve of you."

"I thought you were a grown-up woman who made her own decisions."

"Touché."

He lifted her hand to his lips.

She pulled him close. They kissed again. He ran his hands along her hips. "Careful. Don't wrinkle the dress."

They let go of each other and walked back to the table, hand-in-hand. Zander frowned when he saw them. He ignored Danny and Genie. "I've got to go. Early day tomorrow."

"I'm going to stay a bit," Nadia replied.

"Are you sure?"

"Yes."

"You know what's best."

"I do."

"Want me to leave you the car?"

"I'm drinking. I'll catch a rideshare."

After Zander left, Genie found Becky in the back hall by the kitchen. The sound of dishwashing and kitchen cleanup mixed with the music coming from the bandstand. "Any problems?" Genie asked.

"Piece of cake," Becky replied. She passed her Nadia's phone.

"Wait for me in the car."

Genie went back to the table and knelt down between Danny and Nadia. "I think I'm going to go as well." She dropped Nadia's phone into her purse.

"Okay," Danny said.

Nadia put her hand on Genie's shoulder. "Good to see you."

"We'll have to do this again."

Nadia watched Genie walk away. "She's not going to be jealous?"

"Like I told you, she's not my wife. We're partners. She'll be fine. Another drink?"

"Just one more."

He waved at their server.

GENIE AND BECKY drove to the Hashemi building and parked in the shadows next to the office. Becky laid a tablet in her lap. "I cloned the phone onto this tablet for convenience. Let's see what we've got."

She turned on the tablet and checked the office Wi-Fi. "The signal is strong. We're in. Let me open her computer."

She watched the screen. "Hang on, I've got to break through a firewall. This will take a minute." She cabled the tablet to her laptop, found the program she needed, and clicked on it. "Okay, now I can inject the worm. Just a few more seconds."

She smiled. "There you have it. You're inside her computer. Let me clean this up a bit." She input some code. "Okay, just click on this icon when you want to access her computer. As long as you're on the Wi-Fi, and her computer is connected, you'll be able to see what's happening in real time—email, all the files, passwords, everything."

"Thanks."

Becky unplugged the cable to her laptop. "If the worm is discovered—I don't know how that could happen, it's in deep—but if the Feds get on her machine, find the worm, and start probing, a warning box will come up on the tablet. Turn off the Wi-Fi and the GPS immediately. Then ditch the tablet."

"Gotcha."

Genie drove out of the warehouse district, took the beltway to the north of town, and got off at the airport exit. The traffic was sparse, and the traffic lights were all green. She pulled into the Sheraton Hotel across from the airport and stopped under the awning. "Thanks, again, Becky. Your fee will reach you the usual way."

"Always a pleasure."

Genie popped the trunk, and Becky took out her suitcase and pushed the lid shut. Genie watched her stroll into the hotel. She texted Danny. *All good.*

DANNY AND NADIA were groping each other like teenagers at the door to her townhouse when he felt his phone vibrate in his front pocket.

"Enough," Nadia said, "Let me get the door open." She pulled her keys from her purse and turned to the lock. Danny glanced at his phone and replied with an exclamation point.

Nadia pushed the door open, flipped the light switch, and dropped her purse and keys on the floor. Danny was right behind her. "I think I'm drunk," she said. She kissed him. She was standing so close that he could see the contact lenses in her eyes. "I don't want to give you the wrong impression." She started unbuttoning his shirt. "I'm not the kind of girl who sleeps around."

"I know." He took her in his arms and kissed her. Drunk? She'd had three drinks, tops. She was wanting this, needing this, looking for an excuse. He whispered in her ear. "So we take it easy. Take our time. We've got all night."

She led him up the stairs.

In the morning, he was lying beside her, watching her sleep, when she opened her eyes. He saw her mind flash through the night before to make sense of what she was seeing now. Her mouth started to open. He kissed her. "Good morning."

She blushed. "I guess I'm not going to get any mileage from saying I don't remember what happened."

"Do you think you made a mistake?"

"I don't know yet." She glanced at the bedside clock.

"Do you have to hurry off?" he asked.

"That would be the easy way, wouldn't it?"

"If you had tipped me off, I could have snuck out in the night."

She sat up, pulling the sheet with her. "I didn't mean that." She smoothed her hair back from her face. "God, I must look a fright. I'm still wearing yesterday's makeup."

He tried a nervous laugh. "I get it, Nadia. You feel vulnerable. You're naked, in your own bed, with a man you barely know. Do you want to get dressed?"

"Could you turn around?"

He turned his back to her. The sheet fell to the bed.

"Okay," she said. She was wearing a fluffy white robe. "I'm going to the bathroom. Then I'll make coffee."

Danny picked up his clothes from the carpet and got dressed. Nadia reappeared, her hair pulled back in a ponytail, her face clean. "I've laid out a toothbrush for you."

After he brushed his teeth and rinsed his face, he found her downstairs in the kitchen standing on the other side of the island. "Nice place."

"Thanks. Coffee is almost ready. I hope the beans aren't too stale. I don't really keep breakfast stuff around here, but I could make some toast."

"Coffee's fine."

She pulled her robe tight, then glanced at the coffee machine as if to will the coffee to be ready.

"Nadia," Danny started, using his this-is-sort-of-awkward voice, "it wasn't just about the sex." He looked at the counter between them. "I mean—it was good, I enjoyed it, I hope you did, too—but that's not the reason—the only reason—I came home with you."

"Please, you don't have to say anything."

"I've been hoping for a chance to get to know you, and maybe things moved too fast, but I don't want to take anything back."

"I—" The coffee machine beeped. She poured two cups of coffee and pushed one across the island to him.

He picked up the cup. "Of course, Genie knows I didn't come home last night, but I could tell her anything. And if you don't want your brother to know—"

"I'm not ashamed of you." She reached out with her free hand. "Let's sit."

She led the way to a loveseat facing the window into the back garden. A birdfeeder stood in easy viewing, but it was empty.

"This is hard for me," she began, looking out the window and holding her cup in both hands. "I have to be careful. You know what I mean. It's the same for you. Someone who's not in the game might not understand. And maybe it was too soon, but I wanted you, I wanted you to come home with me. It's just that things are so much easier in the night when you've had a few drinks."

He put a hand on her knee. "So you want to keep going?"

She nodded.

He slid next to her and put his arm around her shoulders. "I'm glad. I know your brother still doesn't trust me, but when he finds out I'm a man of my word, when he sees that I'm not going to hurt you, everything will be easier."

"I hope so."

"How did you end up smuggling for the cartel anyway? Your business isn't a money laundry. It's the real deal."

"Even before the embargo crushed our carpet imports, the bad blood between the US and Iran could make importing difficult, so we'd get pinched at various times. Pauly—my husband—knew a guy who wanted to bring things in through the port. We'd always said no..."

"Until you didn't."

She nodded. "One thing led to another. We finally convinced our uncle to seek out contacts in Uzbekistan and India so we wouldn't have import problems, but by then we were all the way in."

"So your uncle handles the other side?"

"For us. That's the way it's always been. The cartel, on the other hand—we don't know how they get their packages into our shipments." She set her coffee on the end table and put her hand on top of his. "I'm glad you didn't sneak off in the night." She kissed him.

"I'm glad I'm still here."

WHEN DANNY OPENED the door to their rental, Genie was waiting for him in the living room.

"Well?" she asked.

"You aren't going to let me get a shower first?"

"No."

"Becky gone?"

"I dropped her at the Sheraton last night. She flew out this morning. Stop deflecting and give me the dirt."

"Took it from start to finish. She was hesitant and maybe a little embarrassed when she woke up, but I sealed the deal using the I-understand-why-you-don't-want-anyone-to-know angle."

Genie laughed. "Then she really is in love."

"She's been by herself too long. The trust isn't there yet, but she's hoping against hope."

"So how are you going to play it?"

"Like the straight-up boyfriend. Going to show a lot of care. Which reminds me." He took out his phone. "Clare's Florists? I'd like a bright bouquet sent to Nadia at Hashemi Carpets & Arts. Before 2:00 p.m. The card? Can't get you out of my mind." He gave them his credit card information.

"Isn't that a little over the top?"

"No, I don't think so. She's smuggling the cartel diamonds, and we're going to play her, but she may never find out the truth, and she might as well have a nice little love affair."

Genie shook her head. "You're such a gentleman."

.   .   .

NADIA MET Julie for lunch at The Tea Room, a new specialty tea and sandwich shop across the street from the strip mall on Kennedy Boulevard. Julie waved at her from a table about halfway back when she came in the door. "I ordered a pot of the English," she said.

Nadia sat down and glanced at the menu. "Sorry to be late." The menu was salads and dainty sounding sandwiches—cream cheese, cucumber, watercress, shaved ham. "What are you having?"

"I'm going full retro. Cream cheese and cucumber. White cake for dessert."

"I'll have the same. I hope you're right about this place."

"Stacey loved it, and you know how particular she is."

Their server, a middle-aged woman wearing a frilly apron over a simple dress, brought the tea on a tray with cups and milk and sugar.

After their server took their order, Julie said, "You look—I don't know, satisfied isn't the word, but something's up."

"You remember that guy who came up to our table at The Clam Chowder?"

Julie nodded. "Danny."

"I don't know how you're so good with names."

"It's a gift."

"We were at a client dinner last night at Wyatt's Supper Club. Zander went home early, and we ended up on a date."

"A date? With this Danny guy? I told you he was interested. So how did it go? What did you do?"

Nadia opened her mouth as if she was going to speak, but no words came out.

Julie's eyes lit up. "Did you? You didn't—on the first date? You did."

Nadia nodded.

"Wow," Julie said. "At your house? He stayed the night? Oh my God. That's a big step for you."

"It was surreal. But in a good way. For you it's every day—I mean, you're married. But to wake up with a man in my bed, after so long."

"A new man."

"Yes, a new man. The first man after Pauly. It was strange." Her eyes watered.

Julie patted her hand. "But everything's okay?"

"Yeah, I was a little out of sorts."

"Well, of course."

"We had coffee, talked. Then it didn't seem so weird."

"Are you going to see him again?"

"We didn't make another date right then, but he's got my private number. I think he's going to call."

"Nadia, maybe he's the one."

"It's too soon to tell."

"Maybe, but it's never too soon to be happy."

LATER, when Nadia got back to the office, she found a large vase of colorful flowers on her desk. She didn't know what to think. She looked at the card. *Can't get you out of my mind.* She smelled the flowers, taking in their scent. She felt like a girl in a romance novel running across a field in the spring. Could this really be happening to her?

She sat down behind her desk. Careful. The flowers were gorgeous, but what did they really mean? She wasn't a schoolgirl in a romance novel; she was a grown woman in the real world. She couldn't let her emotions get ahead of her. She needed to hold on to her heart until she could really be sure. She looked at the flowers again—the reds, yellows, whites, and greens swirling like an impressionist painting. But in the meantime, why shouldn't she enjoy whatever it was she was getting into? She deserved a little excitement. And wasn't this the way it always began—with the intoxication that led, maybe, someday to love?

Zander stepped into her office. "I see you found the flowers."

She smiled.

"Must have been some evening."

"It was."

"Did things go the way they looked like they were going when I left?"

"He spent the night, if that's what you're asking."

"So you've made up your mind?"

"I don't know about that. I'm just going to figure things out as I go along."

"Do you think that's a good idea when we don't know if we can trust him?"

She rolled her eyes. "I'm not telling him our family secrets, Zander. I'm just hoping for some fun times."

"Look, Sis, I don't want to argue."

"Then don't." She gave him a look that said it was time for him to leave. "Shut the door on your way out."

She watched him go. Was she being foolish? Of course. But was she being too foolish? She didn't think so. Thinking about last night and this morning, she felt so alive. The world felt full of possibility for the first time since Pauly died. Would Danny break her heart? Maybe. Would their relationship go nowhere? Probably. But for right now, she wasn't willing to give up the opportunity to feel those feelings she hadn't felt in so long, and to maybe find the love she'd only known once before.

GENIE WAITED in her car in the far corner of the Walmart parking lot away from the surveillance cameras. At 6:00 p.m. on a Friday evening, the Walmart was in full swing. Some families were pushing full carts out to their cars, while others were hustling into the entrance to buy the week's groceries or maybe just tonight's supper.

Stowe pulled up beside her and climbed into her car. "What's up?" she asked. "Why did you want to meet here?"

"We can't meet at the Bayside Lounge anymore. The cartel guys will be watching for us."

"I thought your people controlled the port."

"That's the whole point. If the cartel guys start pushing their weight around, the union leadership will start worrying about the Feds, and I'll be in big trouble."

"But how much does this cartel guy really know?"

"He knows enough. He knows I took that container. He knows you're involved."

"I thought you knew what you were doing."

"I do know what I'm doing, and that's why we're not doing it anymore."

"Look, me and my partner have an agreement with some folks about lifting certain containers—"

"That's not my problem."

"What do you think is going to happen if we don't come through? These people won't just be coming for us. They'll be after you and your family."

Stowe banged his fist on the dashboard. "What the hell?"

"You liked the money, didn't you?"

"I never should have—"

"Too late for that. You're in. I'm in. There's no getting out. This is what we're going to do. We're going to stick with our arrangement. We're only going to take the containers that we absolutely have to. You'll still get paid and your family will be safe."

"You're a bitch."

"Careful, sugar. That's not the kind of talk that gets you in a girl's pants."

"Fuck you."

"I know you're going to come around when you've had a chance to think it through. Keep your head down. I'll let you know when we need the next container."

Stowe raised his hand as if he might slap her. She kept her eyes locked on his. Instead, he grunted, reached down for the door handle, and pushed the car door open. He looked over his shoulder and muttered a curse she couldn't quite hear, climbed into his truck, and sped away.

Genie reached across from the driver's seat to shut the passenger's door. He was emotional, and that was good. The ones that went quiet were more likely to screw things up. She called Danny and filled him in.

"He almost hit you?"

"He wasn't going to do it."

"He'd have wished he'd smacked his mother if he did."

"We don't need to go there."

"But he's still going to cooperate?"

"Definitely. He stews a few days, he'll know he doesn't have a choice. We just can't use him unless we really need to."

"Shame he got cold feet."

"At least I won't have to screw him anymore."

"Always looking on the bright side. I'll have to tell Zander something."

"Good luck with that. Where do you want to eat supper?"

"Let's meet at home and then we'll decide."

DANNY SAT in a car parked on Fulton Avenue. Nadia was in the Merry-Go-Round bar across the street having a happy hour drink with her friend Julie. He had planned to run into them and ask Nadia out on a date for Saturday or Sunday, something casual and innocent, but he might as well call Zander first. "Zander, there's a problem at the port. Nothing we can't sort out, but we can't take any more containers until its dealt with."

"What kind of problem?"

"The kind of problem you don't want to know anything about."

"Do I need to find another port guy?"

"More players will just make things worse. Let us deal with the problem. We'll have it straightened out in no time."

"I can't wait too long."

"Neither can we."

SUNDAY AFTERNOON, Danny and Nadia were at Havel Pond Park, strolling along the path by the water, watching the ducks dunk and paddle. On the other side of the pond, children rushed around on the soft-surface playground, sliding down the slide and clambering over the play structure.

"How long will you be here?" Nadia asked.

"Generally, we stay somewhere until the action wears out," Danny replied.

"And how long will this action last?"

"That's a good question." He took her hand. "We're having a little trouble at the port. Nothing we can't figure out, but working the port can't last. Too many moving parts for independents like us. Of course, for you, you'll lose your side action, but everything the cartel protects will keep rolling."

"But the money—"

"That's the rub, isn't it?"

"Then you'll go?"

"I don't know. We've also got a little action with your brother, doing things he doesn't want to do. There might be some new game we can get up and running, and between the two, and other considerations"—he squeezed her hand—"maybe we'll be here a long time."

They stopped at a wooden lookout jutting over the pond and stood at the railing. A kayaker scattered the ducks. An older couple walking a golden retriever passed behind them. Danny put his arm around Nadia. "So I can't make any promises."

She leaned her head against his shoulder. "The future is far away."

He nodded.

"So let's live for today. See what happens."

He kissed her lightly. "Ready to head back?"

They started back toward the parking lot. "This is a nice little park," Danny said. "Thanks for suggesting it."

"There's another park, much larger, on the north side of town. You bring your hiking shoes, I'll take you there sometime."

"Want to go to dinner with me?"

"I'd love to, but Sunday night is family night at Zander's." She glanced at her watch. "I do have an hour, if you want to stop by my house."

"You're insatiable."

"I am."

"Ravenous."

"Stop it."

He pulled her close and kissed her. "I'd love to stop by your place."

LATER, when Danny got back to their rental, he found Genie at the kitchen counter, chopping cabbage for a salad. "Hey, honey."

She looked over her shoulder. "How's it going with Nadia?"

"She believes anything I say. I almost feel bad."

"I bet."

"Learn anything from her computer?"

"About the diamonds? Nothing yet. Their financials are solid."

He slipped up behind her, put his arms around her, and kissed her neck.

"I'd have thought you had enough already."

"Of you, baby? Never."

"You're wasting your time trying that sweet talk on me."

He pushed her up to the counter. She pushed back and spun around in his arms. Their faces were inches apart. "You want to play rough?" he asked.

She bit his lip. "You're going to know the difference, sweetie."

"No bruises."

"Softy."

She boosted herself up onto his hips. He shifted her onto the counter and pushed her skirt up.

4

COMPLICATIONS

Monday afternoon, FBI Special Agent-in-Charge Jerome Victor and Special Agent Chris Martinez, currently assigned to the Counterterrorism Task Force, sat down across the desk from Agent Clara Garcia in her office at the National Defense Agency building in Washington, DC. Garcia, a full-figured Latina dressed in a black pantsuit with a white shirt, sat back in her chair and pushed her shoulder-length hair behind her ears. "How can I help you?"

Victor started in. "We've got Fatherland Volk white nationalists talking with somebody from the One World Jihad Union about obtaining uranium."

"You sure it's One World?"

"That's the claim."

Garcia turned to her computer and clicked through some screens. "One World Jihad Union. There's solid intel that they stole a quantity of uranium during the Syrian civil war."

"Jesus. This is real?" Martinez asked. "We thought it was probably a scam."

"Let's see what else we've got on One World." Garcia clicked through some more screens. "Here we go. Come around here where you can see."

Martinez and Victor stepped around her desk.

"This is eyes only," Garcia said. "This picture was taken in a Dublin, Ireland, coffee shop. The guy on the right is Major Javad Tehrani, Iranian Revolutionary Guards. According to our sources, he's got no official reason to be there. The guy on the left is, best guess, Omar Khan of the One World Jihad Union."

Victor cut in. "I thought no one knew what that guy looked like."

"Your tax dollars at work," Garcia replied. "Best guess."

"What's this got to do with us?"

"I don't know. Maybe nothing. But here's Khan, out in the open, taking the risk of being spotted, talking with an Iranian major in an EU country. A major who's involved in clandestine operations. Why would he do that? Something is up."

"That doesn't mean it's got anything to do with Fatherland Volk," Victor said.

"You're right. But this kind of deal would be right up Khan's alley. Blowing up targets in the US. Nobody's done that since 911. Just imagine the press."

"But you're tracking Tehrani?"

"I can't comment on that. You can assume what you like from what I've shown you."

"But if uranium were coming into the US?"

"You'll be the first ones to know of any credible threat."

"Thanks for your time, Garcia."

"You bet."

ON WEDNESDAY, at 6:00 a.m., Zander's burner cellphone rang. He rolled over in bed and grabbed it out of his night table drawer before the sound woke his wife. "Hello," he whispered, as he climbed out of bed and walked out into the hall.

"Hello, Eskander." The voice spoke in Farsi.

"Tehrani? Why are you calling? This isn't our protocol." Zander made his way into the kitchen and turned on the coffeemaker.

"We needed to talk."

"I'm listening."

"Your uncle and his family are being investigated. Some witnesses have come forward questioning his loyalty."

"But we've done everything you asked."

"Maybe it is all a misunderstanding, maybe it is not. Maybe it could all go away. Your cooperation, your friendship, could make all the difference."

"But we've never held back. We've handled every shipment you've given us."

"Now is not the time for questions. Now is the time to do what you are told." Tehrani ended the call.

Zander paced around the island in the kitchen, the phone in his hand, his mind flashing through worst-case scenarios of his uncle being tortured, his property confiscated, his cousins Jasmine and Sara raped in prison.

His wife, Bonnie, came through from the hall, her blonde hair tousled, her open robe trailing behind her. He slipped the burner phone into his pajama pants. "What's up, honey?" she asked.

"Someone called. Uncle may be in trouble. I'm not sure what to do."

"It's the afternoon there. Call him up." She handed him the landline.

He called his uncle's number. The phone rang and rang, but no one picked up. "No one's there."

"In the middle of the afternoon? Call your cousin."

He called his cousin. On the third ring, she answered. He spoke in Farsi. "Jasmine? Where's Uncle? No one answers the phone at his house."

"Well, hello to you, too, Eskander."

"Have you seen Uncle?"

"Not since Sunday. What's this about?"

"I got a call that worries me. See if you can find him. And maybe you should take your kids to the summer house."

"You're frightening me."

"That's because I'm frightened. Call me when you see Uncle." He hung up the phone.

"Well?" Bonny asked.

"Jasmine hasn't seen him."

"Call you sister."

Zander picked up his smartphone from the kitchen counter and speed-dialed Nadia. Her voice still had sleep in it. "Are you alone?" he asked.

"That's none of your business."

"Something's up with Uncle."

"Hold on." A moment later she said, "Go ahead."

He walked back into the hallway away from his wife before he told Nadia what had happened.

"So we don't really know anything. Except that Tehrani wants us to be afraid and to do whatever he asks."

"True."

"So we sit tight, do what we normally do."

"But what about Uncle?"

"We might make things worse if we poke around. How do you know they're not watching us? That this isn't some kind of test?"

"Okay, I hear you. We do nothing until we know more." He ended the call.

When he came back into the kitchen, Bonnie was standing on the other side of the island, stirring milk into a cup of coffee. "Well?"

"Nadia said to wait and see. That we don't know enough to do anything."

"What do you think?"

"I think she's probably right. It's just hard doing nothing."

She poured him a cup of coffee. "Let's sit at the kitchen table and watch the sun rise."

"I've got to get ready for work."

"There's plenty of time."

. . .

WHEN NADIA CAME BACK into her dark bedroom she could see Danny's eyes following her.

"What was that about?" he asked.

"Just business," she said. She shrugged off her robe, slid into bed beside him, and snuggled up close. "You're nice and warm." She rested her head on his shoulder. "Time difference. Sometimes we have to sort out shipping problems in real time."

"And Zander had to call you?"

"We're a team. We always keep each other informed, especially when there's trouble. At least it was almost time to get up."

He kissed her cheek. "Speak for yourself."

"I said *almost*."

ON FRIDAY AFTERNOON, Zander unrolled the final rug from the new shipment of Indian rugs and found the third candlestick. He pressed it down next to the others in the foam lining of the carrying case before he rerolled the rug. These were not jihadi-looted antiques or cartel-stolen items, they were simply objects that could not be legally imported but were on the open market. Three Coptic Christian candlesticks from the early CE. These were the last items Uncle had been able to obtain before he disappeared. The soft glow of the gold, the intricate carving—they were in perfect condition. The collector who'd ordered them was going to be very happy. Zander closed the carrying case and carried it into his office, where Danny and Genie were waiting.

"I appreciate your help," he said.

"Not a problem. Another package for the Oasis Café?"

"No. Here's the address for this one." He handed them a scrap of paper. "Make sure you hand the case to Tommy Berger."

Danny read the paper. "Berger Auctions." He looked up at Zander. "All the way over in Sandy Ford. That'll take almost an hour. It's already four thirty. Will he still be there?"

"He'll be expecting you."

Zander walked them out to their car and watched them drive away. A person couldn't be too careful. Uncle was still missing—probably being held by the Revolutionary Guard, but he hadn't been officially arrested yet. Nadia was right. At this point it was better not to ask questions. But were they being watched here in the US? Was the warehouse or his house or her townhouse under surveillance? The Oasis Café was clean, at least according to Danny, but that was one of Tehrani's drop-offs. If Tehrani was orchestrating this new pressure, maybe he was watching all their activity. Or maybe, worst case, Tehrani had attracted the attention of the US authorities. Maybe Customs was tracking his contacts, maybe he'd been losing shipments and that was why he'd become threatening. Better not to be seen transporting smuggled artifacts. He still didn't trust Danny and Genie, but they were perfect for the job. They weren't connected to the carpet business. If they were arrested, no great loss. Nadia would be disappointed, of course, but she'd get over it. Life would go on. And she'd be spared the greater disappointment of discovering that Danny wasn't the man of her dreams. If only they could be sure Uncle was safe.

DANNY AND GENIE pulled into the freeway rest stop. There were only three cars parked in the passenger vehicle parking, all in front of the entrance to the building. A man with a dog on a leash was walking over by the picnic tables. Danny parked well away from the building, but he kept the engine running. "So why is Zander sending us?"

"He's afraid he's been compromised, and he's less concerned about us seeing his operation than he is about going to jail."

"Why? What's new? He must have confidence in this Berger guy."

"So what do we know?" Genie asked.

"The Oasis Café is definitely an illegal merchandise drop. Probably political, judging from the neighborhood activity."

"Citizens looking out their windows."

"Exactly," Danny said. "Hating the cops more than the local knuckleheads."

"So now he's sending us to Berger. Let's have a look in the case." She opened the case in her lap and turned on the flashlight on her smartphone. The candlesticks glowed in the light.

"Nice looking. Valuable, no doubt. But we could have opened this case inside the rest stop," Danny said. "Customs might care about it, but the local police wouldn't have a clue." He looked over his shoulder. All three cars were still there. "Anyone follow us?"

"No. There hasn't been much traffic. Nobody's tailing us." She closed the case.

"Well, let's get this done."

Danny took the ramp back onto the freeway. Twenty minutes later they pulled into the gravel parking lot of Berger Auctions, a huge, sheet-metal building with a painted sign on the roof, located just off the freeway exit into Sandy Ford. The only car in the lot was a restored mid-1960s Lincoln Continental. "I'm guessing that's Berger's," Danny said.

The front door was unlocked. Rows of dining room tables, dressers, china hutches, and other furnishing ran down to the back of the space. Two oversize garage doors gave access from the back of the building. A section of animal heads—a moose, a longhorn sheep, two elk—hung on the right wall, next to a section of Navajo blankets. An office was situated in the back corner. Danny and Genie made their way down the nearest aisle.

As they approached the office, a short, fat, bald man with a Santa Claus beard came out. He smiled. "Saw you on the camera. Was just finishing up a few things. How can I help you?"

"Are you Tommy Berger?" Danny asked.

"In the flesh."

"Zander Hashemi sent us."

He nodded and then led the way into his office. OD green army surplus desk, matching file cabinet, a four-foot tall floor safe, and three chairs. "No need to sit down." He motioned for the case.

Genie passed it to him. He opened it on the desk, took out one of the candlesticks, and turned it over in his hands, muttering as he studied the engravings. He looked up at Danny and Genie. "Been a long time since I've seen one of these of this quality. Particularly this old. Tell Zander I'll transfer the money into the usual account."

"Will do," Danny replied.

Berger followed them out to the front door and locked it behind them. As they crunched across the gravel to their car, a single pickup truck drove past, the driver with his arm hanging out the window.

"Just a straight-up business venture," Danny said.

"Buy for a nickel, sell for a dime," Genie replied.

"No reason for the cops to be the least bit interested."

"So why is Zander so paranoid?"

"I don't know. Maybe he's just nervous by nature."

"I'll be glad when we have the diamonds."

"You and me both."

MacBurn and Johnston walked up the steps to the Truman Presidential Library in Independence, Missouri. MacBurn wore a khaki explorer's vest and a Panama hat. A camera hung from a strap around his neck. Johnston wore a ballcap and wraparound sunglasses. A busload of tourists crossed in front of them, moving toward the entrance to the building. "This will be the easy one," Johnston said. "Gun the engine, run right up the front steps, crash through the glass into the lobby, and boom."

"Yeah, getting in will be easy. But that's only half of it. It's only a complete success if we get away."

"Surveillance camera on the corner. Lift your left hand like you're adjusting your hat and keep walking."

They continued around the side of the building. "A man could crash through the front and run out through a side door before the explosion. There's plenty of emergency exits," Johnston said.

"Mix in with the visitors and run back to the parking lot."

"That's probably the best."

They walked across the lawn back down to the parking lot where they'd left their truck. "Think Lang could do it?" MacBurn asked. "He's been a lot of help, but he doesn't have a lot of initiative. If he got caught or blown up, he wouldn't be that big a loss."

"I've been thinking about him," Johnston replied. "First, his wife was visiting her mom, then she didn't want to leave her job until she lined up a new one, then he finally admitted that she'd left him. Has anyone seen her?"

MacBurn shook his head. "What are you saying?"

"Maybe he doesn't have a wife. Maybe he just made that up."

"Are you saying he's a plant?"

"No. The guy's been true blue. I'm saying maybe he's gay."

"Gay?"

"Think about it. Even drunk he doesn't flirt with women. He's not a churchgoer. He's supposed to be married, so he's got an excuse for not dating."

MacBurn laughed. "I never thought about that. He acts like a regular guy."

"I'm not saying he's not reliable. A man's private life is none of my business. I'm just saying maybe we need to keep an eye on him."

ON SUNDAY MORNING, Zander drove into Point Jericho Memorial Cemetery, looked at the cemetery map on the seat beside him, and continued up the hill. A thin drizzle was falling—just enough to be an irritation but not enough to require the intermittent wipers. He parked on the side of the asphalt roadway near a freshly dug grave. This was the closest spot. To the east, near a cedar tree, he could see his cartel contact standing at a headstone as if he were visiting a family member, his hands clasped together and his head down. Mr. Wishes was a thin, white man with pale skin, light blue eyes, and white blond hair. He always wore tight-fitting black gloves and a black suit. Zander hated meeting him in isolated locations, because he was always afraid that Mr. Wishes had asked him to meet in such a remote place because he planned to kill him.

Zander climbed the hill through the wet grass and stopped next to Mr. Wishes, looking down at the headstone as if he, too, were paying his respects. "You wanted to see me?"

"The diamonds are in the next carpet shipment, packed the usual way. We know you've been pulling side jobs, that you haven't been paying the tax, but we don't care as long as we're your priority. So don't fuck around. Take care of us first."

"Have we ever let you down?"

"This has to go right. No interference, no cops, no mistakes."

"There'll be no mistakes. If you don't care about the tax, could you tell your guys at the port?"

Mr. Wishes glanced at him as if he were an insect he didn't have the heart to crush and then walked off over to hill. Zander stood for a few minutes, looking at the headstone. Carved roses at the top. *Mary Carter. Beloved wife and mother. Your love will light the way. 1947-1979.* A shiver ran up his back. Thirty-two years old. Too young. Was that Mr. Wishes's—or whatever his real name was —message?

The drizzle was changing into a light rain. Zander turned up the collar on his coat and jogged down the hill to his car. He needed to stop being paranoid. The cartel needed them to move their special items. They must have a reason to keep their own people at the port out of the loop. And as long as that was the case, Hashemi Carpets & Arts would be valuable.

A funeral procession started in the main entrance at the bottom of the hill. Zander glanced at the cemetery map and took the second right turn so that he could leave out from the side exit. He turned on his windshield wipers. What a miserable day for a funeral.

He drove back across town toward the port, turned onto Blue Gill Way, and parked in front of the offices at the Hashemi Carpets & Arts building, where he found Nadia in her office at her computer. "I thought I'd find you here."

"Just catching up a few things."

He closed the door and sat in the chair facing her. "I just saw Mr. Wishes. The diamonds are coming in the next carpet shipment."

She closed the document she was working on and pulled up her office calendar. "Almost six weeks. The Uzbekistan carpets." She put a star next to the Uzbekistan shipment.

"We met at the cemetery."

"Kind of dramatic, isn't it?"

"I told you he's like a guy from a horror movie."

"Well, he's got nothing to worry about. The carpet shipments are always on time."

"All I'm saying is that we've got to be extra careful."

"We always are."

"But now we've got Danny and Genie to consider."

"Meaning?"

"We can't afford for them to mess up this shipment."

"They don't know about the shipment. And you're the one who decided to use them as couriers, not me. Anything they know about our business is because of you."

"I know that, but you're sleeping with Danny."

"Which is your business how?"

"You want to sleep with a guy, sleep with a guy, but what if he finds out about the diamonds?"

"How would he do that? There's no information at my house or in this office that could tell him, or anyone, about a cartel shipment."

"Maybe we need to circle the wagons. Just until after the shipment."

"Zander, I know Danny's a rogue. I'm not a fool. But Pauly has been gone three years. I'm enjoying the attention. I like being with him, and I'm not going to stop just because Mr. Wishes is bullying you."

"He's not bullying me."

"Everything is going to be fine. Anything else?" She turned back to her computer.

Zander left her office. Everything she said was true. There was no way for Danny and Genie to find out about the diamonds unless Nadia or he told them. There had never been a problem with anything smuggled in a carpet shipment. He was the one who'd decided that using Danny and Genie to deliver items was safer than doing it himself. But something was wrong about Danny and Genie. He could just feel it. Danny wasn't Pauly, would never be him, no matter how much Nadia wanted him to be. But something else was bothering him about Danny, something bigger, and he wasn't going to let his guard down until he knew what it was and was sure it couldn't blow up in their faces.

LATER THAT NIGHT, in Nadia's townhouse, Danny lay on his side, drawing slow circles on her back with his finger as they lay together in bed. "How are you feeling?"

She sighed. "Do you even have to ask?"

"So family night at Zander's, what did you do?"

"Bonnie made lasagna. I brought a salad. We ate, played Chutes and Ladders with Tracy—you know, family time."

"How old is she?"

"Seven."

"She's your only niece?"

"Yeah, don't think there's going to be more, but that's okay."

Danny stopped drawing on her, and Nadia propped herself up on her elbow. "Can I ask you a question?"

"Sure."

"Have you solved your problem at the port? Or have you got some other action going on?"

"We've got a few irons in the fire. But that's not your real question, is it? You're wondering if we're planning to move on."

"Yes."

"We haven't made any plans, and I'll tell you if things are going in that direction."

"I know we haven't made any promises."

"You won't be surprised." He smiled. "Unless we're on the run from the cops."

"You're just teasing, now."

He ran his hand up and down the curve of her hip. "Are you having a good time? 'Cause I'm having a good time."

She closed her eyes. "Yes."

"You're a special woman, Nadia. I don't know what's happened to you in the past. I may leave or I may stay, but, either way, I'm not going to hurt you." He leaned up and kissed her softly.

She took his hand.

"Can I ask you a question?" he said. "It's a little more personal than the one you asked me."

"Okay."

"Your husband. What happened to him?"

"Like I said before, business was tight. People would ask Pauly if we would help them get something through the port. Finally we started smuggling. Told ourselves that we would quit as soon as the embargo let up."

"But you didn't."

"No, we got used to the money. And the smuggling was Pauly's thing. He grew up in a rough neighborhood, knew some people, so he handled it all. Zander handled the warehouse. I stayed in the office. It was a perfect division of labor."

"Until?"

"The cartel wanted us to come in with them. We moved a few loads for them, but we wanted to stay independent. Then an out-of-town crew tried to squeeze us. Pauly wouldn't back down, wouldn't go to the cartel. He brought in some friends. For a while, it looked like the out-of-town crew was going to back down." Her voice cracked. "Then a truck Pauly was driving burst into flames." She started to cry. "He burned to death in the cab."

Danny pulled her into his arms and rubbed her back. Her tears trickled down his shoulder. "I'm so sorry," he said.

"It's still hard."

He reached for the tissue box on the nightstand and handed her some tissues. She blew her nose.

"And you haven't dated since?"

She shook her head. "It just seemed so hard to move on." She wiped her eyes. "After that, we went in with the cartel. They dealt with the out-of-town crew."

"So the cartel could have been behind it all. They could have been using the out-of-town crew to pull you in."

"Zander doesn't think so, but I'm not so sure."

"I'm sorry I made you cry."

"That's okay."

"Let me get you a glass of water."

"You don't have to."

"I want to."

He got out of bed and padded through to the kitchen in the dark. So the love of her life was murdered, they're under the cartel's thumb, and they're still pulling side jobs. He filled a glass from the tap. They really were amateurs of the worst sort. It was hard not to feel sorry for her.

ON TUESDAY, while Danny was out with Nadia, Genie sat in her car in the shadow in the alley next to Hashemi Carpets & Arts, her tablet in her lap, going through Nadia's computer. She'd made a copy of the drive early on so that she could do a forensics deep dive, going back through the shipment records, looking for patterns, without having to be parked next to the warehouse. The records were clean, all the shipments accounted for, all the associated paperwork verifying every item in every shipment from the original port all the way to the Hashemi warehouse, which meant nothing so far as any smuggled goods that might be piggybacking on a legitimate shipment.

About half the carpet shipments originated from Mumbai, India, near the diamond trading hub, the carpets coming by truck from handlooms in Bhadohi and Agra, India, and Samarkand, Uzbekistan. And the next Mumbai shipment would be arriving in six weeks. How accurate was Billy's info? Time was getting short, so Genie was double-checking for any changes on the records. The diamond shipments were twice a year. The only anomaly she'd found thus far was that twice a year a carpet shipment originating in Mumbai was marked with an asterisk. And now, looking at the scheduled shipments, the new carpet shipment arriving from Mumbai in six weeks was also marked with an asterisk. Why did that seem strange? She'd been over all these pages until her eyes hurt. Why hadn't she noticed that before? She took a screenshot of the page. She sipped coffee from her Caffeination drive-through cup. What was bothering her?

An SUV pulled up behind her, its headlights cutting through her car. She put the tablet to sleep and flipped it over onto the passenger's seat. She kept her eyes on her driver's side rearview mirror. The SUV looked somehow official. A man in a uniform got out and started toward her car. As he approached, she could see that he wasn't carrying a gun. She smiled to herself. Private cop. He tapped on her window with a large flashlight. She lowered the window and put her hand on the butt of the Glock resting in her door cup holder.

"What's up?" she asked.

"Why are you parked here, ma'am?"

"Who are you?"

"I'm with Ridley Security. This is private property."

"Oh, I see." She frowned. "I'm waiting for a friend."

"You're not allowed to park here. Could you show me some identification?"

"No."

"No?"

"I don't know who you are or why you're here. You say you're with a security company. But how do I know? You could be a rapist. You touch my door handle, you're going to get shot."

"What?"

Genie put her car in drive and started down the alley. The man just stood there, his flashlight pointed at the pavement in front of him. She came out of the alley onto Blue Gill Way, took the next corner, and sped up to gain some ground, just in case he'd rushed back to his SUV and started chasing her. Then she took two more turns in quick succession. No one was following her. Ridley Security must be paying minimum wage.

On her way home, her mind strayed back to the shipping records. What about the upcoming shipment from Mumbai seemed peculiar? What a minute. She pulled over, put in her password on the tablet, and clicked on the original document. There was no asterisk on the upcoming shipment. She looked at the screenshot. Asterisk. She grinned. Nadia must have added it since she made the original copy. This had to be the diamond shipment. She texted Danny. *I know the date.*

    For sure?

    Ninety-nine percent.

    Talk tomorrow.

5

THE FBI

In the morning, after Danny had coffee with Nadia at Rudy's Coffee and Books, he called Genie while he was walking down the block to his car. "Did I wake you?"

"No, I was brushing my teeth."

"Sleeping in?"

"Sleeping alone."

"I think I'm going to cry."

"You're an asshole."

"I've already had my coffee." He looked at his reflection in a storefront window. "So when is the diamond shipment?"

She explained what she'd found out.

"I like your thinking, but I wouldn't call it ninety-nine percent."

"Ninety, then."

"Good enough to start deciding how we're going to do the job."

"Now you're talking."

"So the security guy rolled right up on you?"

"Doesn't really matter now. We don't need to hang around there anymore."

. . .

THAT AFTERNOON, Zander walked across the warehouse, his phone up to his ear, and stopped in front of a shelf of rolled carpets. "Yeah, like I said, I've still got one from Uzbekistan in the size you want. I can email a picture."

"That would be great."

"This is the last one of this quality. After it's gone, I won't get any more like it until the spring."

"I hear you."

"Okay. I'll send the picture."

He ended the call and started toward his office. His smartphone rang. He answered without looking at the number. "Hello?"

"Hello, Eskander." It was Tehrani's voice, speaking in Farsi.

Zander stopped and glanced around to make sure he was alone. "You shouldn't be calling me on this phone."

"Your uncle has been arrested."

"Uncle? On what charge?"

"The charges could be complicated. They could involve national security."

"That's insane. My uncle has never been involved in politics."

"Listen. A special package will be included in the Mumbai carpet shipment. After this package is given to the courier, the charges against your uncle will be dropped."

"Why are you threatening us?"

"Pay attention. The Mumbai shipment. The package goes to the courier." Tehrani ended the call.

Zander banged his fist on a work table. These bastards. When would it end? They never showed any respect. What could possibly be in this package that was worth Uncle's life?

He hurried from the warehouse and down the hall to Nadia's office. She looked up from her computer. "What's up?"

He closed the door and filled her in.

"So now we know where Uncle is," she said.

"He's in prison."

"But now there's a record. Before they could have murdered him and no one would have known. Now they have to at least make up a reason."

"That doesn't sound much better. And this special package. I'm worried," Zander said.

"I know. Why tell us it's special? If we didn't pass it along as usual, Tehrani could put us out of business, disappear all of our relatives. There's no need."

"Unless whatever it is is so terrible that he's afraid we won't move it unless the threat of ruin is hanging over our heads."

"We need to find a way to protect ourselves. We need more information. What about some of Uncle's contacts? Do you know any of them?" Nadia asked.

"I haven't spoken to any of them in years." He started going through the contacts on his smartphone. "What about Assad? He still helps us every now and again if we have a licensing problem."

"Call him."

"On this phone?"

"It will look like a normal business call to a government office."

He tapped on Assad's phone number. The phone rang four times before Assad answered. He put the phone on speaker and spoke in Farsi.

"Assad? This is Eskander."

"You're lucky I hadn't left yet. Why are you calling me?"

"Uncle is missing. Major Tehrani called today. He said Uncle has been arrested. Can you find out what's going on?"

"What have you gotten yourselves into?"

"Nothing. I swear. You know us. We don't want any trouble. We always cooperate with the authorities."

"Okay, I'll make some discreet inquiries. But I won't get involved."

"Of course not."

"And if I find out you're not telling me the truth, you won't hear back from me."

"I'm telling the truth."

"Very well. I'll call when I know something. Probably a few days."

"Thank you."

Zander ended the call. "Now we just wait."

"No," Nadia said. "We need a plan."

"What do you mean?"

"Like you said, this package must contain something really bad—something that's not a looted artifact, something we wouldn't want to be involved in. So what is it? Poison? A weapon? How far are we willing to go?"

"To save Uncle's life?" Zander replied. "As far as we have to."

"Let's say what's in the package could kill two people. Would you do it?"

"We're not talking about killing anyone."

"But if we were? You know Tehrani. He's capable of anything."

"Hypothetically? Two strangers against Uncle and our cousins? No contest."

"One hundred people?"

"Sis, that's just crazy."

"We know it's bad. But how bad? Moving an object that's already been stolen is one thing, but moving something else, something dangerous . . . How far are you willing to go?"

"We don't know what's in the package."

"But when we do?"

"I don't want to make a decision that I might not have to make," Zander said.

"So you want to wait?"

"We need more information. We should at least wait until we hear back from Assad before we do anything."

"This problem isn't going away."

"I know. But we're only talking about a few days. Let's wait until we know what Uncle's situation really is."

IN WASHINGTON, DC, Clara Garcia sat at her desk in her office at the National Defense Agency, going over some files, waiting for a secure video satellite uplink to come in on her desktop computer. One of their deep-cover agents in Iran had information on Tehrani that couldn't wait for the monthly summary. When the call came through, she was looking at a middle-aged man with a short, gray beard who was wearing a mullah's turban.

"What have you got for me?" she asked.

"Tehrani picked up a guy named Amin Hashemi. He's half of a carpet-and-antique business. The other half of the family business is in the US."

"What did the guy do?"

"That's why I called. Hashemi hasn't been arrested. His family is searching for him. He's been stashed somewhere. And Tehrani is supposedly on vacation."

"So he's on a mission so secret that his office can't know."

"Exactly."

"Send me your full report."

"Sending it now."

"Keep me updated."

"Yes, ma'am."

Garcia closed the uplink, opened the secure file, and scrolled down to the US connection, Hashemi Carpets & Arts in Point Jericho. She googled the website. Two smiling American faces standing in front of a wall of rolled carpets. Zander Hashemi and Nadia Hashemi Wright. Importers of the finest handcrafted Indian and Uzbeki carpets. Usual sales pitch.

She called Special Agent-in-Charge Victor at the Counterterrorism Task Force. "Garcia here. On the uranium smuggling, I maybe have a lead for you."

"I'm listening."

"Tehrani is putting pressure on a family that imports carpets into the US."

"How?"

"Disappeared their uncle in Iran."

"Can you sent me the file?"

"It's on its way."

"Thanks."

. . .

TWO WEEKS LATER, Special Agent Chris Martinez and his seven-person team were on the ground in Point Jericho. They were operating out of a shuttered plastics extrusion warehouse three blocks south of the Hashemi Carpets & Arts building. Video and voice surveillance had been set up on the warehouse. They were just waiting for the court order. Two-person teams were tracking Zander Hashemi and Nadia Hashemi Wright, photographing and taping everywhere they went in public. A stingray device—a cellphone tower simulator—had been set up in a utility van parked in front of a self-storage unit across the street from the Hashemi building so they could tap the Hashemi's cellphones when they were at their business.

So far, Martinez's team had zilch. The background investigation had turned up nothing substantive. No tax problems, no arrests, no personal issues. Their extended family were Iranian citizens. Nadia Wright's husband, Paul, had died in a truck fire. Zander and Nadia came to work, they went to lunch with friends, Zander went to his daughter's after-school activities, and he went home to his family in the evening. Nadia went to dinner and then went home with a man who seemed to be her boyfriend, even though he'd been renting a house with another woman for the last few months. These two were Caucasians with no connections to the immigrant community. They appeared to been completely normal citizens, except that they had no pasts. They just sprang from the ground in Point Jericho. So they were either with some other government agency—Homeland, DEA, ATF—or they were dirty.

Martinez called Garcia. "Are you aware of any other undercover operations going on in Point Jericho? Anything outside the task force?"

"Why?"

"There's a couple associated with the Hashemis who don't seem to have a past."

"Do you have a photo? I can push it through the database."

An email came through with the photo attached. Garcia opened it. A man and a woman in a driveway next to a Cadillac. This couldn't be right. She rubbed her eyes, blinked, studied the photo. It was the grifters from Mitchellville. The Kyrgyzstan case. What names had they used then? She leaned back in her chair, thought about the last time she'd seen the man. It was winter, in Kickapoo Creek. He'd been going by the name C.D. Abbot. She looked at the photo again. It was definitely him.

"Martinez?"

"Yeah?"

"These two are professional thieves."

"Really? Tied up with the Hashemis?"

"Keep an eye on them, but keep your distance. If they see you, they'll bolt. I'll be in Point Jericho tomorrow."

THE NEXT DAY, Martinez was sitting in a blue Subaru waiting for Garcia outside the baggage claim at the Point Jericho Municipal Airport. When she came through the automatic doors, pulling a wheeled overnight bag, he got out of the car and opened the hatchback.

"How was your flight?"

"Uneventful."

He took her bag and put it in the back. "Why are you so interested in our ghosts?"

"Because they only work big money jobs. If they're here, something's up."

They drove down Martin Luther King Drive, heading south into town.

"The local cops know you're here?" Garcia asked.

"No."

"Have you got a secure location where we can question them?"

"We've got a motel room."

"The couple. What names are they using?"

"Danny Briggs and Genie Pullman."

"Do you know where they are now?"

"Yes."

"Pick them up. Be discreet. If things work out, we want to be able to throw them back."

DANNY AND GENIE had gotten up late, eaten a leisurely breakfast, and taken their time getting ready for the day. Now that they had a probable solid date on the diamond shipment, they couldn't afford any side jobs complicating their efforts, so all they had to do was maintain their covers while they set up the actual theft.

When they finally left the house at 10:00 a.m., two unshaven men wearing work clothes got out of a beat-up Ford Bronco parked on the street and fast-walked up the lawn toward them. As they approached, the nearest one held up an FBI badge.

Danny held his hands out away from his body. "Gentlemen," he said.

"You're coming with us," the nearest man said.

"Gee," Genie said, "I wonder what we've done."

"Shut up."

They cuffed them behind their backs, put them in the back seat of the Bronco, and drove out to a Budget Inn at the freeway interchange, where they pulled into an empty space in front of room 124. "No police station?" Danny asked.

The driver spoke into his phone. "We're here." Then he turned to his partner. "Take him. She stays."

The other man pulled Danny from the back seat and led him into room 124. There were two people standing in the room—Clara Garcia and a suit who was probably FBI.

"Sit down," Garcia said.

The undercover agent pushed Danny down in the desk chair.

"Garcia," Danny said. "You're the last person I expected to see."

"Do you know why you're here?"

"Are we going to have a philosophical discussion about God and the nature of the universe?"

"I didn't think you'd get in bed with terrorists."

"What terrorists?"

"So who's your target?"

"You know I'm not going to tell you that."

"For the record, I don't care which crooks you rob. But the Hashemis—your new best friends—are planning to smuggle a package into the US for a terrorist group. We want to know when it's coming, who takes delivery, and where they go. You're going to help us with that."

"No."

"Think we don't know all about the theft at the port? Customs is on top of it. We've got you, your wife, the union guy, and the Hashemis dead to rights. We can toss you back into the game or drive you straight to the county jail."

"What if you're wrong about the Hashemis? What if they're just moving regular old contraband?"

"They're not. But if they are, you better hope you find out something that you can trade."

Danny looked from Garcia to the suit and back again. "So if we help you with the terrorists, we can play our game and walk straight up out of here?"

"That's the deal."

Danny gestured toward the suit. "What about this guy. He's the FBI, right?"

The man in the suit nodded. "The deal is good with us until we have the package we're looking for. After that, it's back to cops and robbers."

"Handcuffs?" Danny leaned forward. The undercover agent uncuffed him. Danny looked at his watch. "If you want to have your way, you need to drop us back at the house. I have a lunch date with Nadia."

Garcia nodded toward the man in the suit. "From here on out, Martinez is your contact. You won't see me again if you keep your word."

Martinez handed Danny a cellphone. "When it rings, you answer it. When you know something, you call me. My number's in the phone."

"Gotcha."

"You focus on staying out of jail, and we'll play nice." He turned to the undercover agent. "Take them back to their house."

Danny and Genie didn't speak until they were standing in the front yard of their rental house, watching the undercover agent drive away. "So?" Genie asked.

"We can assume our house and the cars are bugged."

"That bad?"

He filled her in on his conversation with Garcia.

"So Stowe was even a bigger idiot than we thought."

"Evidently."

"Hard to believe Zander and Nadia are hooked up with terrorists," Genie said. "They don't seem like the type."

"I know, but Uncle Sam doesn't have to be right."

"Time to run?"

"No. Garcia is a ballbuster, but her word's good. We'll have to tiptoe around the FBI a little bit, but I think we can stall long enough to get the diamonds. It's only three weeks."

"Closer to four. And no matter what they said, you know the FBI will try to bust us as soon as they have their package."

"Then the diamonds better come first."

THREE UTILITY VANS sat side-by-side in the red barn across the gravel access road from the Lang farmhouse. Bruce MacBurn and Joe Lang were using a pump syphon to transfer diesel fuel from the tank of a diesel truck into a fifty-five gallon steel drum.

"How many more after this one?" Lang asked.

"Ray says two more," MacBurn replied. "This one is full." He turned off the syphon and pulled the hose.

Lang screwed in the plug. "Would have been a lot easier to just get the big diesel tank filled instead of driving back and forth filling up this truck at different gas stations."

"There's no equipment storage here, is there?"

"No, that's all up at the renters."

"So how would you explain it?" MacBurn asked.

"I know, I'm just saying."

"Do the job right, we stay out of jail."

"And then we've still got to load the fertilizer," Lang said.

"That'll be the easy part. Just take a farm truck to the Coop."

"But Ray is sure he can get the C-4?"

"Don't worry about it. Ray's the man."

"I'd just hate to do all this work for nothing."

"You won't be. Folks will be talking about this project for a long time to come."

"Longer than Oklahoma City?"

MacBurn chuckled. "Is anybody still talking about that? Let's get out of here. It's time for a cold one."

They slid the barn doors shut. MacBurn locked the padlock. They glanced around. There was no one driving by on the nearby county road, and the only noise was the buzzing of the insects in the uncut hay. MacBurn looked toward the one-story farmhouse across the access road. "How's your granddad?"

"Still at the care center. My mom says he'll never leave."

"Sorry to hear that."

Lang shrugged. "It's all up to God."

"What's your wife think about it?"

"Don't know. I haven't heard from her."

LATE IN THE EVENING, after his children and his wife had gone to bed, Zander was sitting in the den, drinking a beer and watching TV, when he got a call on his smartphone. "Hello?"

"It's me," a voice said in Farsi.

"Assad. Good to hear from you."

"I contacted a few people. Your uncle hasn't been charged with anything. Tehrani is—what would you call it—moonlighting."

"Are you sure?"

"Absolutely. I can get your uncle released, but it will take time."

"This is the best news. If you ever need a favor—"

"I know." Assad ended the call.

Zander called Nadia. "Can you talk now?"

"Yes."

"Assad came through. It's just a matter of time."

"That's wonderful."

There was a pause on the line. "Are you still there?"

"Yes," Nadia said. "I was just thinking. We never should have agreed to help Tehrani. All these little packages. We knew they were stolen artifacts."

"But we didn't know where they came from."

"We could guess. All the news stories about war-zone thefts. And we knew who we were delivering them to."

"We were protecting our family."

"We should have helped everyone to emigrate. Then we couldn't have been blackmailed. Instead, we turned a blind eye."

"Well, Uncle is safe. We just need to keep our heads down."

"And what do we do about the special package?"

"Maybe Tehrani will be demoted."

"You don't really believe that. Tehrani is going to expect us to move that package. This is our country. Could you sleep at night knowing you helped do something terrible? Even if it was to save a family member?"

"Nadia, you're overreacting. We don't know what's in that package. We just know it's important."

"Then what is it?"

"Just wait. Uncle will be safe and we'll be able to put all of this behind us."

AN HOUR LATER, Martinez was sitting in his office in the plastics extrusion warehouse drinking coffee and going over some paperwork. Agent Jennifer Ables, dark blonde hair, glasses, dressed like a factory worker in jeans and a sweater, knocked on his open door. "Yeah?"

"Moving the stingray to Hashemi's house paid off," Ables said.

"Here's the transcript. The first call is from Iran. We'll have it translated by morning. The second call is in English."

Martinez read through Zander and Nadia's phone call. "This is good stuff. Did the court order come through?"

"Not yet."

"We'll have to chalk this up to a confidential informant."

"But now we know we're on the right trail."

"Maybe. The Hashemis are under pressure to smuggle an object. It must be happening soon. But is it the uranium?" He handed her the transcript. "Get in touch with Customs at the port. We need to make sure that nothing is getting in or out without our knowing about it."

"I'll get it done first thing in the morning."

After she left, Martinez called Danny. "I interrupt your beauty sleep?"

"What do you want?"

"Looks like we were right about the Hashemis. Your girlfriend is having second thoughts about smuggling the package."

"How do you know?"

"How do you think?"

"You want me to flip her?"

"Find out what we need to know."

6

MAKING A DEAL

Two days later, Danny and Nadia were in bed in the dark in her townhouse. It was their usual midweek date. The bedroom door was cracked open and the hall light was on, a shaft of light cutting across the bottom corner of the bed. Danny was kissing her and moving his hands over her body, but she wasn't responding. "You're not here."

"Work problems," Nadia replied.

He rolled off her and turned on the side table lamp. "Something's up, and it's more than a bad day at the office."

"I'm not sure I should tell you."

"Baby, we're sleeping together, and we're doing crime together. Whatever you won't tell me scares the hell out of me."

"You're a player?"

"You know it."

"How far would you go?"

"On a scam? All the way."

"Even if innocent people will get hurt?"

"You mean civilians? People not in the game? You've got to keep them out of it. What's this all about?"

"You've seen we have two kinds of side jobs."

"The antique dealer and the Oasis? Yeah."

"The packages that go to the dealers, that's money in our pockets. But the packages that go to the Oasis Café, well, that's a different thing."

"What do you mean?"

She looked for his eyes. "Can I trust you?"

"You know you can."

"We have to move those packages to keep our relatives safe."

"In Iran?"

She nodded her head.

"And something's come up."

"There's a package coming that I'm worried about."

"Why?"

"Because they kidnapped our uncle to make sure we'd deliver it."

"And they've never done that before?"

"No, never. In the past, I always thought the packages were looted antiquities. Stuff being sold to finance jihadis somewhere else. To tell the truth, I never really thought about it. We just moved them, and our family was left alone. But now…"

"So you figure this new package must contain something different."

"It must be horrible. Why else would they threaten us? They must think we'd refuse to move it if we knew what it was."

"So what do you want to do?"

"I don't know. I can't think straight. I just don't want anyone to get hurt."

"What does Zander think?"

"He thinks we should just keep our heads down, not ask any questions, hope it all blows over, and then make a plan to protect our family."

Danny didn't respond.

Nadia put her hand on his shoulder. "Danny?"

"I was just thinking—there's a guy we know who might be able to help."

"A guy?"

"An FBI agent who's been helpful to us from time to time."

"Someone who works with you?"

"It's complicated. We do each other favors. I could reach out to him if that's what you want."

She sighed. "I won't get Zander into trouble."

"Of course. Maybe he's right. Maybe if you just sit on it, this problem will go away."

"You don't believe that, do you?"

"It's not what I believe. It's what you believe. Which is worse? What are you willing to live with?"

"God, God, God. The FBI—"

"Not the FBI, a guy I know."

"I just don't know."

"Talk it over with Zander. Decide what you want to do, and then get your story straight so you're only telling my guy exactly what you want to tell him."

"Let me think about it."

"Sure."

"Could you turn off the light?"

Danny turned off the side table lamp. She spooned up against his chest. He felt her deep exhale as he held her close. She'd made her confession. She wasn't holding the secret anymore, so she was free to make up her mind. She was stronger than her brother. She'd get her way with him. Tomorrow or the next day, she'd be ready to go to the FBI. And then he and Genie would have Martinez off their backs.

IN THE MORNING, Danny found Genie in the kitchen of their rental. She glanced over her shoulder with the coffee pot in her hand. "Thought that sounded like you coming through the door. Want a cup?"

"Please."

She poured him a cup of coffee. They sat at the kitchen table. Through the backyard, they could see a youngster swinging on a swing set in the neighbor's backyard. "Tell all."

He filled her in.

"I like it," she said. "You get Nadia connected with Martinez, and then the FBI are focused on them, and we've got more running room to grab the diamonds and pull our disappearing act."

Danny nodded. "There's an eighty percent chance the diamonds are in the next carpet shipment."

"Eighty percent? It's higher than that."

"Eighty, ninety—it's all the same. With a little bit of luck, the diamonds will be there, and we'll already be gone when the terrorist package arrives."

"Long gone. Whether or not the package is what the Feds are really looking for, they won't be able to arrest us for the port jobs," Genie said.

"And as long as the FBI is hovering, the cartel will have to tiptoe around Nadia and her brother."

Something in his tone of voice brought her up short. She looked at him quizzically. "Why do you care what happens to them? They're criminals, not civilians."

"But they're entirely clueless. There's nothing wrong with them getting a chance to make their escape after we take the diamonds."

She took his hand. "Honey, you're not getting attached to her, are you? Because if you are, that's okay. You've been spending a lot of time with her. You've just got to be honest with yourself and with me."

"I'm fine."

"Okay."

"I'm good to go. I know whose team I'm on."

"I believe you. Just had to ask."

NADIA TOOK her time showering and getting dressed. She was glad Danny had hurried off when they got up. She wanted her privacy this morning. Telling Danny about the package had been the right thing to do, but she still felt anxious, out of her depth, not ready to deal with moving the special package and its possible repercussions. Pauly would have known what to do. He was a hard man. Sweet to her, a friend to her brother, and hard to the rest of the world. The irony was that if Pauly had been alive, they never would have ended up under Tehrani's thumb. Tehrani never would have trusted an American. But Pauly had been killed. They were already smuggling. Zander couldn't see a reason not to help. Of course, they were already fearful that more bad things could happen to them. So they ended up with the cartel on one side and Tehrani on the other side, and there they were in the middle, being squeezed. Uncle was safe this time, at least according to Assad. But maybe Danny's FBI friend could deal with their Tehrani problem without putting Uncle or their cousins in any future risk.

When she got to their offices, she found Zander alone in the warehouse standing at the carpet rack, inputting information from a group of rolled carpets onto a tablet. "Hey, Sis."

"Getting a shipment ready?"

"Loom Arts in Chicago called. They want the ten carpets we've been trying to get rid of for the last six months, so I'm getting them ready."

"Can I talk to you?"

"If I can keep working."

"I talked to Danny about our situation."

"You told Danny about Uncle?"

"Yes."

He stopped what he was doing. "Are you insane? Everything has to be kept in its own compartment. We agreed. The Tehrani compartment. The cartel compartment. The side job compartment. Information spilling back and forth is going to lead to trouble."

"We've already got trouble."

"No, we don't. It's already taken care of. All we have to do is wait for Uncle to be released."

"That special package is trouble. You need to take your blinders off. If we don't find a way out, we're going to end up as accomplices to something terrible."

"So what did your new boyfriend have to say?"

"He's got an FBI agent he knows."

"A guy like him?"

"Yeah, someone who's helped them out in the past."

"Great. A crooked cop. Somebody else to get in our pocket."

"I'm not going to let this go, Zander. Moving stolen antiquities? Okay. Moving looted antiquities that are maybe going to fund terrorism somewhere else? Not so okay, but if that's what we have to do to protect our family, I'm not going to fight you over it. But this? I couldn't live with myself if any innocent people were hurt because of me. Could you?"

"Nadia, what kind of man do you think I am? I don't want anyone to get hurt. But going to jail or putting our family at risk is not going to help."

"Maybe this FBI agent could deal with Tehrani without putting us at risk. Maybe we'd never have to smuggle for him again."

"You're grasping at straws."

"We have to do something. Tehrani is just going to keep demanding more."

"We don't know what's in this package."

"Except it's worth kidnapping Uncle to guarantee our compliance."

"So I can't talk you out of this?"

"No. I'm going to meet with Danny's friend. Test the waters. See if a deal is possible."

"Don't talk in specifics. Don't admit to anything."

"I won't."

"Okay. See if a deal's possible. But that's all."

Nadia took out her smartphone. "Hey, Danny," she said.

"What's up?"

"The guy we talked about?"

"Yeah?"

"Give him a call."

LATER THAT AFTERNOON, Lang sat at his desktop computer in his bedroom, keeping an eye on the road in front of the farmhouse while he talked on a secure video link with Agent-in-Charge Victor. "Mac-Burn and Johnston just got back from scouting the Denver mint. That was the last of them."

"So it's definitely the Denver mint, the Truman Library, and Wright-Patterson Air Force Base."

"Yes. MacBurn is getting the blasting caps this week. Johnston is reaching out to someone for the C-4, but he hasn't heard back."

"I'll contact ATF and see if we can't get control of that situation."

"We still haven't heard anything about the uranium, but MacBurn says we won't hear from the jihadis until they're ready to deliver."

"Have they recruited the drivers?"

"I don't know. They're keeping me out of the loop on that. As the time approaches they're becoming more suspicious."

"But no one knows old man Lang?"

"Nobody. He's had Parkinson's for years."

"And your cover is holding up?"

"I think they're becoming a little concerned that there's no way to check my backstory. It wasn't supposed to hold up so long. They're particularly curious about why my wife has never turned up."

"But you've got control of the materials?"

"The vans, the fertilizer, and the diesel fuel are all right here in the barn."

"And there's no plan to move them?"

"Not that I know of."

"Anything else?"

"No. I'll be in touch as soon as we hear from the jihadis."

THE NEXT AFTERNOON, Nadia and Danny were sitting in his Cadillac in the parking lot of Oceanside Park, well away from the other cars that were parked closest to the beach access, when Martinez pulled in beside them in a green Subaru and got into the back seat.

"Hey, Danny," he said.

"Hey, buddy," Danny replied.

Martinez turned to Nadia. "So you're Danny's friend?"

Nadia nodded.

"I understand you've got information about a possible terrorist attack?"

"Maybe. Let's talk in hypotheticals first."

Martinez smiled. "Go on."

"If someone had valuable information, but needed to remain anonymous, how would you handle that?"

"We'd interview the subject, verify all the details, and then attribute the info to an anonymous source."

"But you could guarantee this person's safety and immunity from prosecution? No one would find out about their involvement?"

"Absolutely. We could keep the whole thing hushed up. And if we have their full cooperation, we could guarantee immunity, but only for crimes connected with the investigation."

"I see."

"It's the best offer you're going to get."

"I have to think about it."

Martinez got out his business card and wrote a phone number on the back. "That's my private number. I'll answer twenty-four seven."

Nadia took the card. "I'll be in touch."

"Don't wait too long. The farther down the road things go, the less I'll be able to do for you."

Martinez got out of the back seat. They watched him drive away. Danny patted Nadia's thigh. "That wasn't so bad, was it?"

"No, it wasn't." Nadia studied Martinez's business card. The phone number on the back was written in a right-leaning scrawl. She slipped the card into her purse. "Makes you paranoid, though."

"Dealing with the FBI? It better." He put the Cadillac in gear. "You have to go back to work?"

"Yeah. I want to get this over with."

"You think Zander will go along?"

"He has to."

"You want me to go in with you?"

"I better go in alone."

. . .

NADIA FOUND Zander in the warehouse with two of their warehouse workers, pulling rolled carpets from the racks to assemble an order for shipment. "Got a minute?" she said.

He nodded. He handed his clipboard to one of the workers and pointed at the list with one finger. "Here's where we're at."

They walked through to her office. After he shut her door, he said, "So?"

She filled him in on her meeting with Martinez.

"You're buying this?" he asked.

"Yes, I am. There's nothing to tie us to any of our other side jobs, no paper work, nothing. We tell Martinez about all of the Tehrani jobs, anything he wants to know, we say we were afraid for our relatives, we were duped—"

"You think they'll believe that?"

"It's true. Pauly was dead. We were afraid."

"I don't know, Sis, I just don't know. There's no walking back from this step. We'll have to give up our side money."

"I've thought about that, too. But, come on, we make good money from our business. And we're not cut out to be crooks. Not without Pauly."

"We're not crooks."

"We've been smuggling contraband. That makes us crooks. That's why we're being jerked around by Tehrani and the cartel, and we can't do anything about it."

"Okay, I hear you, but that doesn't mean we should tell the FBI. If Tehrani or the cartel find out, we're dead."

"Tehrani's not going to find out. The FBI needs to cover their tracks if they're going to trace the terrorists. They have to make it look like somebody else screwed up. And the cartel's not going to find out. It's got nothing to do with them. We'll move their product just like always."

"You hope they won't find out. We'll end up buried in a state park."

"They won't find out. They don't know about any of the side jobs that are hidden in carpet shipments."

"This plan is still crazy."

"Of course it's crazy. But when the terrorists do whatever horrible thing they're planning, do you think for a minute we won't be found out? Homeland Security, the FBI, who-knows-what will be digging under every rock. It will be like 9/11 all over again. And as soon as they find us, we'll end up at some nightmarish black site. Is that what you want for Bonnie and Tracy?"

Zander held his hands together as if he were praying. He let out a long sigh. "Okay. You're right. Call him. I just hope this isn't a mistake."

"You sure?"

"Yes."

THAT EVENING, Nadia and Zander sat in office chairs at a long folding table in what had once been the break room at the shuttered plastics extrusion plant. Martinez and Ables sat across from them. Ables had a legal pad in front of her and a pen in her hand.

"Can I get you anything?" Martinez asked. "Coffee? Water? Diet Coke?"

Nadia and Zander both shook their heads.

"Okay, then," Martinez continued. He turned on the recorder on his smartphone. "It's Saturday, October 15, Chris Martinez and Jennifer Ables, Counterterrorism Task Force, interviewing confidential informants. You've got some information about a possible terror attack?"

"Let's hold up a minute here," Zander said. "We need to start with the specifics of how you'll help us."

Martinez turned off the recorder. "As I told your sister earlier, if we have your full cooperation, we guarantee immunity from prosecution, but only for crimes connected with the investigation."

"And no one will find out we helped you?"

"That's right. We need to chase down all the possible suspects, so we can't have them knowing where the information came from."

"How do we know you'll keep your word?"

"You'll just have to trust me."

Zander turned to Nadia. "Maybe we need a lawyer. Maybe we need official paperwork outlining a deal."

Martinez leaned forward, putting his elbows on the table. "Let me explain how that will work. You can lawyer up. We can Mirandize you. You'll be charged with smuggling and terrorism. You're US citizens working as enemy agents. That makes you traitors. Is that what you want?"

"You don't have anything on us."

"Please. Customs has a case on you, Danny Briggs, Genie Pullman, and Charlie Stowe. We start pulling on that thread, how far do you think it will go?"

Zander's mouth fell open.

"Look, we've got an ongoing investigation that we think you may be part of. That's the only reason we're sitting here. We arrest you, you get a lawyer, everything's public, you still tell us everything in a few months. But we don't have a few months. Innocent lives may be at stake. You haven't been Mirandized, so nothing you say can be used against you in court. Tell us everything you know. You'll stay safe. The smuggling case will go away. You'll do your part on the war on terrorism."

Nadia put her hand on top of Zander's. "This is our only chance."

Martinez turned on the recorder. Nadia and Zander told him everything about their relationship with Tehrani.

"So Tehrani—a major in the Revolutionary Guard—is using your uncle as leverage to make sure you'll deliver this particular package, and he's never done that before?" Martinez asked.

"Exactly," Zander said.

"Even though you've delivered other contraband?"

"We assumed it was contraband—stolen artifacts or antiquities—from the sizes of the boxes. We never looked in the packages," Nadia said.

"And you always delivered them without making any complaint?"

"There was always the implied threat that he would harm our family in Iran."

"So what makes this package different is that the threat is actual?"

Nadia nodded. "He must think we won't deliver it if we know what it is."

"But you have a friend in the Iranian government who says he can get your uncle released?"

Zander cut in. "Not really a friend, but yes, he can get Uncle released because he hasn't been charged with anything. He's just not sure when."

"Then why have you come to me?"

"Because it's about more than getting our uncle released," Nadia said. "If they're planning an attack on the US, we don't want to be part of it."

"Okay, when will the package arrive?"

"Soon. We don't know the exact date yet."

"But it will be hidden in a carpet or artifact shipment?"

"Yes."

"Where will you take it?"

"It depends," Zander said. "Sometimes I take them to the bus station, sometimes to the Oasis Café—"

"That coffee shop down in Little Beirut?" Martinez asked.

Zander nodded. "Sometimes someone picks it up."

"You're always the courier?"

"Yes."

"And the pick-up guy?"

"Always different. Always dressed like an American."

Martinez turned off his smartphone recorder. "You're going to go about your business. As soon as you have any new information, you're going to call me, ASAP."

"What are you going to do?" Zander asked.

"We're going to get ready for the next phase. That's all you need to know."

Agent Ables drove Nadia and Zander back to the Hashemi Carpets & Arts building. When she got back to the plastics extrusion factory, Martinez called her into his office. "What do you think about their story?"

"Could be the uranium, or it could be an infiltration we didn't know about. Either way, it looks promising."

"I agree. We need surveillance on the bus station and the Oasis Café."

"We need more people."

"Can we piggyback on any existing security cameras? We're not going to get more help until we have more evidence."

"I'll see what we can do."

AT 10:00 P.M., Danny met Nadia and Zander at the Lazy 8 truck stop out by the east freeway interchange. Several semitrucks were idling in the parking area between the gas pumps and the truck wash, but the restaurant was only half full. The sign by the hostess station said *Seat Yourself*. They sat in a booth against the far wall, Zander and Nadia facing Danny across the table.

"Why did you want to meet out here?" Zander asked.

"Because I don't trust the FBI. Either of you been here before?" Danny asked. They shook their heads. "So we're safe here for now."

Their waitress, a sturdy redhead with gray showing at her roots, came to their booth. They ordered coffee.

After she turned away, Zander said, "An awful lot of coincidence here."

"Such as?" Danny replied.

"Your FBI friend was already on a terrorism case."

Danny shrugged. "There had to be some reason he wanted to meet."

"And he's got us all dead to rights for smuggling out of the port."

"He told you that?"

"You didn't know? He said you and Genie and some guy named Stowe."

"How would I know? I'm in as deep as you on that—deeper, because I met the port guy and drove the truck."

"That's enough," Nadia said. She turned to Zander. "Danny didn't turn on us."

"You don't know that. Not for certain."

"I do."

Danny cut in. "Did Martinez offer you a deal?"

Nadia filled him in on what happened at the meeting.

"So you're all set. Congratulations."

"Unless they find out about some other crime," Zander said.

"Some other crime?" Danny replied. "Martinez is not going to look if you hold up your end. Particularly if you're right, and he gets to break open a terrorist conspiracy. That would make his career. He'll be dreaming of his perfect future as soon as his head hits the pillow."

"Do you really believe that?"

"You've just got to watch yourself. Don't give him any reason to think that you're holding out on him."

Zander glanced at his watch. "I've got to go. Bonnie will be wondering where I am."

"What are you telling her?" Danny asked.

"Nothing, like it's any of your business." Zander slid out of the booth and hurried out of the restaurant.

"Your brother is pretty angry," Danny said.

"It is a pretty big coincidence," Nadia replied. "Your FBI friend being on the Counterterrorism Task Force and knowing about the smuggling at the port."

"But you know better."

"Zander is just a little paranoid right now. Even if we weren't friends—"

"Lovers."

She smiled. "Lovers. You wouldn't set yourself up. You and Genie would have been long gone before the meeting."

"So how do you feel about your situation?"

"I'm feeling better. Still worried. A lot could go wrong with the delivery or right after that could make Tehrani suspicious."

"But it'll be the FBI's problem."

"But it still might blow back on us."

The waitress laid their check down. Danny examined it and put some money on the table.

Out in the parking lot, they stood together just to one side of the glass doors to the truck stop. The night was clear, and a cool breeze gusted toward them from the pumps, carrying its gasoline smell. She stepped up next to him and took his hand. "You coming over?"

"You sure you want me over?"

"Yes, I am."

He kissed her lightly. "I'll meet you there."

He watched her get into her car before he opened his car door and climbed in. He got out his smartphone and called Genie.

"Hey, baby."

"Hey baby yourself. What's the verdict?"

"It all went to plan. They're working for the FBI."

"No drama?"

"Well, Zander's still suspicious, but that's probably as much because his sister's falling in love with me as it is me being so helpful."

"So you got your wish. Now they've got the FBI standing between them and the cartel."

"Maybe."

"Where are you?"

"On the way to Nadia's. Don't think I'm going to get much sleep."

"Please. Your life is so tough."

"Talk to you in the morning."

"Love you."

"Love you."

DOUBLE TROUBLE

Monday morning, Martinez called Special Agent-in-Charge Victor to fill him in about his interview of the Hashemis. "This is promising," Victor said. "We know that Tehrani met with Khan. And here he is blackmailing the Hashemis to smuggle a particular package. It might not be the uranium, but it's definitely something."

"We need to coordinate with ICE at the port."

"I'll make the arrangements when it's time."

"Thanks."

"Keep the pressure on the Hashemis."

"Everything they've told us matches our surveillance tapes."

"So they're playing it straight?"

"They seem to be. If they weren't tied up with Briggs and Pullman, I'd have no doubts."

"We need to be ready when this package gets here."

"We will. We're putting everything in place right now."

"Anything else to add?"

"No."

"Tell me about Briggs and Pullman."

"They don't want to help us, but they're doing what they're told.

He pushed Nadia Wright into our arms. Told her we were friends. Got the conversation rolling."

"And his woman?"

"She's got some union guy at the port under her control. He thinks he's having an affair. That's how they were targeting containers."

"But they're not committing any crimes now?"

"According to Garcia, they specialize in robbing criminals, but we've been on them twenty-four seven, and they don't seem to be up to anything."

"But she's definitely a honey trap, and he's definitely playing Nadia Wright's boyfriend?"

"Yes."

"Remind me of what our deal is with them."

"They help us with the terrorist problem, we forget about the smuggling charges. They don't snitch on regular criminals. That's what Garcia set up."

"Pretty generous."

"I know, but that's what she thought we needed to do to get them on board."

"Lang needs a wife for a few days to burnish his cover. Make sure his associates continue to believe in him."

"We don't have any women with that kind of undercover experience on our team."

"I know. And there's not enough time to find someone. What about using Pullman?"

"You want to use Genie Pullman?"

"You say she's a professional liar and seductress."

"She is."

"So she could easily fool the Fatherland Volk people."

"But she's a criminal."

"We use criminal informants all the time. We need Lang to be above suspicion and right in the middle of this conspiracy. She won't learn any particulars, so her presence won't contaminate the evidence. All she has to do is fly in, make an impression, and fly out."

"I don't think it's a good idea, but it's your call."

"I'll email you the details."

"Okay."

"Keep me up to date." Special Agent-in-Charge Victor ended the call.

WEDNESDAY AFTER LUNCH, Martinez went over the email he'd received for Agent-in-Charge Victor before he called Agent Ables into his office. "Jennifer, have you set up the surveillance of the bus station and the Oasis Café yet?"

"We're on the bus station security cameras, but the Oasis is in a dead zone. The closest cameras are at a Seven-Eleven two blocks away and a grocery store at the intersection with the boulevard."

"But you're on them?"

"Yes, sir."

"Pull in the teams that're tailing the Hashemis. Use them to keep an eye on the Oasis and to set up the sting at the Hashemi warehouse. We're out in the open with the Hashemis now. We'll keep tabs on them via the stingray and audiovisual surveillance."

"What about the port?"

"Customs is already set up. We're going to coordinate with them."

"Anything else?"

"Find Genie Pullman and bring her here."

An hour later, Ables led Genie into Martinez's office. "Sit," he said.

She plopped down in the chair facing his desk, her legs spread and her arms folded like a teenager in the principal's office. "What do you want? And why isn't Danny here?"

"You enjoying our arrangement?"

"What do you mean?"

"It's time for you to earn your keep."

"I don't work for you."

He moved his hand back and forth like a pointer. "In jail. Out of jail. In jail. Out of jail. What's it going to be? You said you'd help, so now you're going to help."

Genie sighed. "You cops are all the same—feds, state, local. You've only got one tune."

"Only need one tune."

"What do you want me to do?"

"You're going on a trip. I've got an undercover agent who needs a wife to show her face for a few days."

"You can't send a female agent?"

"I don't have to. I've got you. No one's going to suspect you of being a cop."

"Ha, ha."

"Exactly. You're leaving Friday morning. Agent Ables will pick you up at 9:00 a.m. She'll have your airline tickets and your new driver's license. Pack for three days."

AFTER ABLES DROPPED Genie off at the rental house, Genie stood in the yard next to her Toyota and watched her drive away. Then she called Danny. "We have to talk."

"Meet me at Oceanside Park."

Danny was already sitting on a bench overlooking the beach when Genie parked in the lot. The tide was coming in, the waves low, washing up into the loose, dry sand. She sat down on the bench beside him before she filled him in.

"Fucking Martinez. This isn't part of the deal."

"It is now."

Danny looked off in the distance for a moment. "Let's back up. Why send you? Why take the risk?"

"They must be understaffed."

"That's an advantage for us. Gives us a little more elbow room. What else do we know?"

"The Feds are waiting on a package. It's got something to do with a terrorist threat. They used you to rope in Nadia and her brother."

"So is this trip where you play house part of this same case?"

"I see where you're going. Can we find out anything that will help us stay out of the terrorist case, collect the diamonds, and get away clean?"

"Exactly."

"Only three days. That's not much time."

"So you'll have to judge the situation just right. Nympho or trusted colleague?"

She laughed. "Maybe nympho and trusted colleague."

"With any luck, this guy's been undercover a long time, lying to everyone until he almost believes the lies. He wants to hold someone close, tell the truth, have someone see him for the hero he thinks he is."

"I'll do my best."

"I know you will."

FRIDAY MORNING, Danny and Genie were ready when Agent Ables arrived. They all stood in the living room. Genie was dressed to travel —tan jacket and slacks, baby-blue shirt, touch of makeup. Danny was unshaven, his hair disheveled, his white T-shirt hanging over his slacks.

Ables handed Genie a manila envelope. "Airline tickets. A brief description of your role. And your driver's license."

Genie shook the driver's license out of the envelope. "Utah. Chrissy Lang."

"Time to go," Ables said.

Danny hugged Genie. "Don't do anything more than you have to." He kissed her.

Genie and Ables left, Genie pulling her carry-on bag. Danny watched them get into Ables's car and drive away. Had he fooled Ables? Had he planted the idea that he felt helpless? Would she report to Martinez that they were fully in charge?

. . .

ON THE PLANE, Genie read over her role. Chrissy Lang, sales rep manager, estranged wife of Joe Lang, hadn't been out to Iowa since Joe moved back a year ago. Joe's picture showed a sturdy working man—he was supposed to be a guy down on his luck who was trying to become a farmer. She, on the other hand, was dressed for success. She rolled her carry-on bag out of the Des Moines airport and onto the sidewalk in front of baggage claim.

Lang, old jeans and a hoodie, stepped out of a white F-10 pickup truck idling at the curb and waved at her. "Chrissy!"

She smiled as she started toward him. He was staying in character.

He stepped around the truck and stopped up short, as if he wasn't sure he could hug her. She pecked him on the cheek.

"How was your flight? I'm so glad to see you."

She played along. "Got upgraded to business."

"Let me get that." He swung her carry-on into the truck bed and then held the passenger door open for her before he jogged around the truck and climbed in.

"So you think they're watching you at the airport?" Genie asked.

"Someone might see me, tell someone they know. All the pieces of the puzzle have to fit together. What have you been told?" He pulled away from the curb.

"I'm your pissed-off wife. I'm going home on Sunday. I don't know why the hell you want to take up farming when you don't know anything about it."

He chuckled. "I like your tone. The guys I'm tracking are all white nationalists. Don't act surprised when they talk racist, but you don't have to—in fact, it would be better if you didn't."

"No problem. What have you been told about me?"

He glanced at her for a second. "The truth? That you're a confidential informant. You're practiced in deceit, and you can't be trusted."

"They didn't pull any punches, did they?"

"This is how the weekend is going to go. I won't be telling you about anything that you don't need to know. Tomorrow morning we'll go for breakfast at the local diner. Everyone will see you. We're going to look like a couple that's trying to get reacquainted."

"I understand. It's breaking-up-is-hard-to-do. We want to get back what we had, but it's not going to happen. So I'm not flirting with the other guys, or even paying much attention to them."

"That'll get the job done."

"It's a walk in the park."

"Then after breakfast we go on some errands, small talk you into the picture, one of my guys will probably turn up at some point, and then we'll play it by ear."

Two hours of driving later, they were parked on the gravel in front of the Lang farmhouse. A single porch light lit the steps. The sky was huge with stars.

"This really is the middle of nowhere," Genie said.

"Makes it a great place to plan a conspiracy."

"And what are they conspiring?"

"That's outside your need-to-know. Chrissy Lang wouldn't know, so you don't get to know."

They went into the house. The living room had a river rock fireplace and two old sofas. Old family pictures hung from the walls. Genie shook her head. "This place is out of central casting."

"Belongs to Brian Lang. He's been in a care center with Parkinson's for years. He's supposed to be my grandfather. That's why I could turn up here."

"And nobody knows?"

"All the people who would remember him are dead, in a care center themselves, or gone to live with their own kids."

"Sad."

"Yep." He led her into the 1980s kitchen. A small table sat near the back door. "Come on through to the bedrooms."

From the kitchen, a hall branched off to two bedrooms separated by a small bathroom. The bedrooms had faded wallpaper and dark-stained trim. One was lived in, one was not. "Yours is the empty room. The bed is probably okay."

"Your friends wander freely in the house?"

"Of course."

"So anyone going to the bathroom could look in the bedrooms."

"What're you suggesting?"

"I'll keep my bag in your room during the day, drop some dirty clothes on the floor, just in case anybody peeks." She rolled her bag into the empty room. "Good night."

ZANDER KISSED his daughter Tracy on the cheek and turned out the lamp on the nightstand beside her bed. "Good night, my darling."

He glanced into the family room. His wife, wearing her furry robe and the bunny slippers, sat in her recliner reading a book. He continued into the kitchen, opened the freezer, and took out a pint of ice cream. He lifted the lid. It was over half empty, so he didn't bother with a bowl. He just grabbed a spoon from the utensil drawer. His burner phone buzzed while he was in the hall. He turned back to the kitchen and put the tub of ice cream down on the counter. "Yeah?"

Tehrani spoke in Farsi. "The special package is in your next shipment."

"The next one? The one in two weeks."

"Yes. Do what you're supposed to and your uncle will be safe." Tehrani ended the call.

Zander sat down in the kitchen. His mind was swirling. The special package and the diamonds were in the same carpet shipment. The one out of Mumbai. If he told Nadia about the package, she would tell the FBI. Which they had to do if they wanted to stay out of jail. But if the diamonds were confiscated, the cartel would certainly kill them. Why, why did everything have to be so difficult? He went to the drinks cabinet and poured himself a whiskey.

Just then, Bonnie came into the kitchen. "Did Tracy enjoy her new book?" She saw the ice cream on the counter and the whiskey in his hand. "What's up? Who was on the phone?"

"Uncle was arrested. We've been trying to get him released."

"Why didn't you tell me? How long has this been going on?"

"A few days."

She put the lid on the ice cream and put it back in the freezer. "You have seemed preoccupied. So that's why you and Nadia have been talking day and night?"

He nodded. "The authorities are maddening. If Uncle had just become a US citizen back when Dad asked him, we wouldn't be having this trouble now."

"But your uncle is going to be all right?"

"I hope so."

She patted his shoulder. "I'm going to bed." She pointed to the whiskey. "Don't drink too much of that."

She shuffled off down the hall. Hashemi sat down at the breakfast table. It couldn't be worse, could it? Tehrani, the cartel, the FBI, Uncle still in custody. Well, he might as well get it over with. He called Nadia on his smartphone. "Can you talk?"

"Yes."

He told her about Tehrani's call. She sighed. "So you told Bonnie that Uncle was arrested?"

"I wasn't thinking. I didn't want to explain the details."

"Well, we don't want her to find out the truth, that's for sure. No more talking now. I'm too tired to think. We'll talk tomorrow, and then we'll tell the FBI."

He looked at the screen on his phone. She'd hung up. Why? *We'll tell the FBI tomorrow.* Were their phones already tapped? He gulped his whiskey. One mistake and they'd be dead. Had Danny thrown them a lifeline or an anchor?

EARLY THE NEXT MORNING, Zander and Nadia were sitting at a tiny table in the back corner of Rudy's Coffee and Books, hiding in plain sight, coffee and bagels in front of them. Rudy's was still mostly empty, the two counter employees handling a stream of to-go orders from the downtown sales crowd.

Nadia sipped her latte. "So the special package will be hidden in the next carpet shipment along with the cartel diamonds?"

Zander fidgeted with a piece of his bagel. "That's our current problem."

"Let's walk through our options. We have to tell Martinez. We have to cooperate."

"What about Uncle?"

"Maybe Assad will come through, and he'll already be free," she said.

"Tehrani can't find out we helped the FBI."

"Agreed. And Martinez doesn't want that. He'll want Tehrani to keep smuggling, so that they can flush out his network."

"You hope," Zander said.

"So Tehrani doesn't find out, and he keeps his word. Uncle is free."

"Why should he keep his word?"

"Because he wants us to cooperate."

"And the cartel?"

"As long as the FBI doesn't know, it shouldn't be a problem."

"Are you insane? We have to tell Mr. Wishes. Maybe he'll want to change things up."

"And maybe the cartel'll kill us when we tell them about the complications," Nadia said.

"What do you think Mr. Wishes will do if we lose the diamonds, and we didn't warn them?"

"Okay. But we're not going to tell Mr. Wishes that the FBI knows about the other side jobs."

"Definitely not," Zander replied.

"We're not going to tell the FBI about the cartel. And we're not talking on phones or at work about anything that the FBI doesn't know about."

"What about Danny?"

"He doesn't know anything about the diamonds, and he's not going to know. So we're agreed?"

Zander nodded.

She got out her smartphone and called the number on the back of Martinez's business card. "Yeah?"

"Agent Martinez?"

"Ms. Wright. What's up?"

"The special package will be in a shipment of carpets that is due to arrive in two weeks."

"How do you know that?"

She told him about Tehrani's call to Zander.

"Excellent news. We'll need the ship name, container number, GPS tracking info."

"I can look up that info when I get into the office."

"I'll be expecting your call."

Nadia put away her phone. "So now you have to meet with Mr. Wishes. You want me to go with you?"

"No. But if I disappear, run."

"I'm not going to do that. I'll put the FBI on him. I'll make sure your family is safe."

BACK AT THE shuttered plastics extrusion factory, Martinez sat back in his office chair and smiled to himself. The Hashemis had decided to give their full cooperation. The phone call to the unknown phone at the Hashemi residence had been too short for the stingray to lock onto, but Nadia Wright's account of her brother's call exactly matched the stingray transcription that sat on the desk in front of him. He'd already informed Agent-in-Charge Victor. The Counterterrorism Task Force was putting together a planning meeting with representatives of the National Defense Agency, ICE, and the ATF. They were going to follow this smuggling network wherever it led, and if this package wasn't the uranium, maybe they'd find it somewhere else in the network.

OUT IN THE country north of Summerville, Little Jo's Diner was situated at a crossroads opposite the Penman Consolidated School. It was a traditional diner, with a row of booths along the windows and a long counter with stools facing the short order cook's station. By 9:00

a.m., half the booths were occupied with retirees sipping coffee and gossiping. Joe Lang and Genie slid into an empty booth near the door. Their plump waitress, her brown uniform already stained with breakfast, grinned as she set down coffee cups.

"Hey, Polly," Lang said. "Yes, please. Both of us."

Polly poured them coffee. "I know what you want, Joe, but I'll be back in a minute to give—"

"My wife," Joe said.

"—your wife a chance to look at the menu."

A sixtyish man wearing a ballcap on his bald head swiveled in his booth to have a look at Genie. "Hey, Joe," he said.

"Hey, Fred."

"Don't usually see you on a Saturday."

"Errands in town."

Fred turned back to the other guys in the booth.

Polly came back and took their order. They made small talk, ate their bacon and eggs, were noticed by the people who were coming or going. An hour later, they were back in Joe's truck.

"That went extremely well," Joe said. "Fred Griswold makes the rounds all day. I bet we're going to be his big news."

"Where next?"

"Ace Hardware."

THAT AFTERNOON, Zander sat at a concrete picnic table facing the parking lot at the first rest stop on the interstate north of Point Jericho. The wind was up, rustling the leaves on the trees, and he could hear a dog barking in the distance. Several cars were parked in front of the welcome center, and people were going in and out of the building. He watched Mr. Wishes get out of a gray utility van and cross to the picnic table, where he sat on the opposite side.

"So you've got a problem," Mr. Wishes said. "What is it?"

Zander told Mr. Wishes about the special package and the FBI.

Mr. Wishes glanced around as if he was making sure he wasn't in a trap. "We knew you had side jobs going, we just didn't think you'd be stupid enough to bring the Feds down on yourselves."

"The Iranians put our uncle in jail."

"Not our problem."

"If you could change your shipment—"

"It's too late for that. You're not dragging me into your mess. You call me to pick up the diamonds after you've gotten rid of the Feds. I don't want to hear from you until they're gone. This is your problem. You solve it." Mr. Wishes pushed himself up from the table.

Zander watched him trudge across the grass back to the utility van and drive away. It was more or less what he expected—the problem pushed back on his plate. At least he wasn't dead yet.

Back in town, he met Nadia outside Wonderful Nails Salon. The downtown parking was already mostly empty except for in front of the restaurants. Dark clouds had rolled in with the wind, and it looked like rain. They walked down the sidewalk as if they were going somewhere. "Well?" Nadia asked.

"No go. Mr. Wishes said it's on us."

"He's been warned."

"I think he thinks we've been warned," Zander replied.

"Okay, we'll just have to keep the FBI from finding out."

"How?"

"We've got to unload the container."

"Because we don't want them to damage the carpets?"

"That's not a reason they'll care about."

"How about because we know where the hiding places are? We can find the package quicker, give them more time before the contact arrives."

"That sounds better," Nadia said.

"Then we can ignore the carpet with the diamonds inside. We find the package and get the FBI off our backs."

"Mr. Wishes shows, takes the diamonds, and we're in the clear." A slow rain started to fall. "Let's get back to our cars."

. . .

LANG AND GENIE were sitting at a table in Clyde's Place, a white nationalist hangout on a wooded hill outside of town. Four men and a woman, all wearing work clothes, sat at the bar. The jukebox played country songs from the 1960s and 1970s. Lang and Genie had been in there for an hour, nursing their beers, hoping to run into one of Lang's Fatherland Volk associates.

"I guess we're done here," Lang said.

"I need to go to the ladies," Genie said.

"Back around the other side of the bar."

She walked passed the customers at the bar and pushed the door marked Women. It was a single-user restroom, not dirty, but messy, with paper towels on the floor and a smeared mirror over the sink. The toilet was clean. She locked the door, peed, washed her hands. As she came back around the bar, she saw two men sitting with Lang, a tall man with a mustache and a crewcut and a fat man with a short beard, and fresh beers on the table. Her chair was still open.

As she sat down, she could tell that both men were drunk. Lang said, "Chrissy, this is Ray," indicating Mr. Crewcut, "and his cousin Jimmy," pointing to Mr. Shortbeard.

"Pleased to meet you," Ray said. He drank from his bottle. "I was just telling Joe, here, about how surprised I was to hear that you were visiting. I mean, he's been home a year, and this is your first time."

Genie acted put-out. "I don't know how it's any of your business."

"Don't get your nose out of joint, Betty. I just said I was surprised."

"Chrissy."

"Oh yeah, Chrissy." He looked at Lang. "So what's the deal? You wouldn't sign the divorce papers, and she had to hand-deliver them?"

"We're just spending time together."

"Sounds good." He turned to Genie. "You planning on moving home?"

"I don't know what I'm going to do."

He took another pull from the bottle. "What do you think, Jimmy?"

Jimmy shrugged.

"This is supposed to be his wife, and I bet he couldn't tell us the color of her underwear."

"You're drunk," Lang said. "And you're getting out of hand."

Ray leaned forward to look Lang in the eye. "You think I'm some kind of Nickletown nigger who can be fooled by this horseshit."

Genie scraped her chair back from the table. "See, Joe, this is why I can't be around you. You think these assholes are your friends."

"Admit it," Ray continued. "You don't like women."

"I'll be in the truck." Genie hurried out of the bar.

"Why did you have to do that?" Lang said.

"Because I don't believe for a minute that she's your wife."

"Fuck you, Ray."

Lang followed Genie out into the parking lot. He could see her standing next to the truck, her arms folded and feet set as if she were angry. He pressed the fob to open the truck doors. She got in the truck before he crossed the parking lot.

"I sure didn't expect that," Lang said.

Genie smirked. "Was he angry because he thinks you're gay and hiding it, or because he's gay and was hoping you were gay, too?"

Lang stifled a laugh. "Well, if he thinks I'm gay, he's not going to think I'm a cop." He put the truck in gear and backed out of his parking space.

"Do all of them just toss around the N word wherever they're at?"

"When they're in a safe place."

"So they really are racists."

"Welcome to America. You can believe whatever you want so long as you don't break the law."

"What put you onto this group?"

"Online chatter. They were doing the kind of research that made it worthwhile to check them out."

"And you've been here a year?"

"Thought I was done after I infiltrated the group for a month. Then they started buying guns. One thing led to another."

The power poles and the soybeans flew by in the dark. He turned off the blacktop onto a gravel road to take the shortcut home.

"So do you really have a wife?"

"Divorced. I was in the military before this. It was just too much."

"Kids?"

He shook his head.

"Do you want any?"

"Got to find a woman, first." He pulled into the gravel driveway and rolled up to the farmhouse. "What about you?"

"It's just me and my partner."

"Until you land in prison."

"We've done all right so far."

Lang unlocked the door and turned on the lights. "Beer?"

"Sure."

He got two bottles of beer from the refrigerator. "It's not too cold out. Want to sit on the porch? You can see the night sky here. One of the few advantages to living this far out."

"I'll get my jacket."

They sat on the glider on the porch, listening to the crickets and watching the occasional headlights speed by on the distant blacktop.

"I'm surprised the crickets are still out."

"It's been a warm October."

She glanced up into the sky. "Is that a meteor?" She pointed up to her left.

"I don't know. Could be a satellite."

She started to take a drink when her eye caught headlights off toward the highway. "Is that car slowing down?"

"It is."

The headlights started down the gravel road toward the farmhouse and then disappeared. Lang rushed into the house, flipped off the light switch, and came out onto the porch with a pair of night-vision binoculars. He trained them on the gravel road and then followed the road back toward the highway until he found a Jeep creeping toward them.

Genie stood up. "Where are your guns?"

Lang handed her the binoculars. "It's Ray's Jeep."

She looked through the binoculars. "I could walk faster than that."

"Yeah," Lang said. "He's trying to sneak up on us."

"Is this his idea of a joke? Sneak down here and then pound on the door?"

"Never done it before."

"He wants to see if we're in bed together."

"You're probably right."

"Right now, he thinks we're turned out the lights to go to bed. Let's not disappoint." Genie led him through the house to his bedroom. They kicked off their shoes and pulled off their jackets before they climbed into opposite sides of Lang's queen-size bed with their clothes on. Genie scooted toward the middle of the bed.

"Don't be shy," she whispered. "Now's the time to seal your cover."

Lang shifted toward her. They lay there, side by side, listening as hard as they could for any rustling in the tall grass outside the window or any labored breathing that could be a drunk moving through the dark.

There was a bump against the siding below the bedroom window. Genie rolled on top of Lang, taking both his hands in hers, and kissed him hard. He moved to push her off, but she locked her legs around him, causing him to flip her onto her back. "Pull up the covers," she whispered into her ear, "so that he can't see our clothes if he's looking in."

She kept kissing him and thrusting against him. He started thrusting back.

RAY JOHNSTON TURNED off the headlights on his Jeep as he approached Lang's farmhouse. He parked at the end of the driveway and sat for a few minutes, listening to the insects. He hadn't been nearly as drunk as he'd pretended to be at Clyde's. He turned off his inside lights before he eased open his door. He slipped around the side of the farmhouse in the dark, not risking even a penlight. When he was nearly under Lang's bedroom window, he tripped over a piece of junk and fell against the side of the house. *Jesus Christ.* He leaned there, listening for footsteps, but what he heard sounded like sheets rustling. He gripped the window sill and lifted himself up. They were in bed together, in motion under the blankets, their faces locked together. He dropped to the ground. He wasn't a Peeping Tom. Maybe he'd been wrong. Maybe she was his wife. Or maybe he was gay and didn't know it. Maybe he was trying to fool himself and her. Johnston crept back to his Jeep, closed the door softly, and inched a hundred yards down the gravel road before he turned on his headlights.

GENIE COULD FEEL Lang hard against her through her clothes. Was Ray still out there? Did it matter? Lang had been a gentleman since the moment he picked her up at the airport. He hadn't tried to flirt or "accidentally" touch her. He hadn't tried to peek when she was changing clothes with the bedroom door ajar. He wasn't screwing around with any of the local women, which was why his buddies had trust issues. So he was an all-around good guy. Maybe she could use that to her advantage. She slipped her hand down into his pants.

"Whoa," he whispered.

"You going to tell?" She kissed him. "'Cause I'm not."

"This is crazy."

"Yes it is. The whole damn thing. Kiss me and unbutton my shirt."

BACK AT POINT JERICHO, Danny and Nadia sat kitty-corner to each other at a table in the back of Little Italy, a wine bar in a strip mall on the west side of town. Their server had just brought their drinks. "So Tehrani contacted you?" Danny asked.

"Yes," Nadia replied. "He called Zander last night. I told Martinez about it this morning. The special package will be in our next carpet shipment."

"When's that?"

"In the next two weeks."

"Wow. It's coming up fast. How do you feel about your decision now?"

"I'm glad I told the FBI, but I still don't like dealing with them."

Danny sipped his wine. "That uneasy feeling never goes away, does it?"

"Exactly." She glanced around the room. "That's why we're hiding out here."

"Wine's good."

"I reported exactly what Zander told me. Do you think Martinez is bugging us?"

"Your phones, your houses, your office? Before you talked to him, you couldn't be sure. But now? Definitely. He knows you have solid info. Why should he trust you? And if you hold back, then he's got a crime he can charge you with. He's probably bugging me and Genie as well."

"So Zander and I need to keep quiet about everything except the special package?"

"I would."

She put her hand on top of his. "Good thing they already know about you."

"How was your day otherwise?"

"Just the usual. Business is good. We added a new retailer in San Diego. They're moving carpets we've been trying to get rid of for months. We'll need the next shipment when it comes in. What about you?"

"Trying to make a new friend at the port. It's delicate work. We have to sneak around our current guy and the cartel. And Martinez is squeezing us."

"Because of that container?"

"Yeah. He claims Customs has us dead to rights, but I don't believe him. It's just been easier to cooperate and wait him out. But now, with your news—in two weeks he'll be gone, finally, and we can slowly ease back to doing our thing."

"Sorry I got you involved."

"Please, I didn't have to connect you with Martinez. I chose to do that."

Their server approached the table. "Another drink?"

"Let's go home," Nadia said.

Danny looked up at the server. "Bring us our check, please."

LATER, at the farmhouse, after Genie went to sleep, Lang lay beside her in the dark, watching her. Victor had been right, she was a top-notch operator. The transition from lying in bed to pretending to have sex to actually having sex had seemed entirely true and natural. Keeping mentally sharp while she was weaving her spell had been a challenge. A few more drinks and he might not have been up to it. Still, the sex had been fun, if unexpected, and he was glad of it. It had been a long time. Too long. Maybe they'd get in another round in the morning if she thought there was still a chance of picking his brain before he took her to the airport. He rolled over to face away from her. He could only hope that she didn't give up too easily.

8

THE LAST FEW DETAILS

Danny met Genie at the airport in the late afternoon. "I missed you," he said. He gave her a hug and handed her a note. *Assume the car is bugged.* They made small talk while he drove out to Prescott Beach. "Let's go for a walk. Get your blood flowing after the plane ride."

They strolled along on the hard-packed sand just out of reach of the waves, the wind blowing into their faces. "I've got news, but I want to hear yours first," Danny said.

She told him about everything she'd done. "White nationalists," Danny said. "What has that got to do with Iranian smuggling? It's got to be connected somehow. Lang didn't tell you anything?"

She shook her head. "No. Racists with guns planning to take over the US. That was it. Pillow talk didn't amount to anything. All he knows about is his end. What's been going on here?"

"The next carpet shipment—the one from Mumbai. It's got the special package in it."

"For sure?"

"Yes."

"So if we're right about the diamonds, they're in the same shipment."

"Nothing's ever easy, is it?"

"The FBI will have the port locked down."

"Definitely," Danny said. "They'll be tracking the ship before it docks. The containers are stacked, so they won't actually be able to see the Hashemi container. They'll be following it using the GPS container tracking system until it's pulled out and loaded on a truck chassis."

"So maybe I can use Stowe to get to the container before it's loaded."

He shook his head. "We can't use him. There'll be cameras everywhere. Besides, the carpets will be folded and rolled. The diamonds were probably loaded in India with the carpets, so best guess they'd be rolled up inside a carpet. Who knows how many of the carpets we'll have to unroll to find them? Can't do that at the port."

"Wouldn't the special package also be rolled inside a carpet?"

"Assuming the diamonds are in there, the package couldn't have been added at Mumbai. The cartel would have been all over that. So the package had to be added somewhere else later. Maybe it isn't wrapped so well."

"Maybe it's close to the front," Genie said.

"The FBI will want to get control of the package as quickly as possible, but they'll also want to set up their sting. So they'll keep everything undercover. The container will go to the Hashemi warehouse."

"Nadia and Zander will want to be in charge of the search. They'll want to find the package as quickly as possible, but not let the FBI find out about the diamonds."

"And the FBI won't leave until after the terrorists pick up the package."

"So the diamonds are going to stay hidden until then."

"We have to get the FBI to take Nadia and Zander with them."

Genie nodded. "And we don't know when the cartel guys are going to show up, so we'll have to move quickly."

"It's a tight timeline all right. The one upside is that if the FBI have Nadia and Zander in custody, it'll make things a lot more difficult for the cartel. They won't be able to talk to them until the FBI turns them loose."

"Gives us time to run."

"Exactly," Danny replied. "One day, two days before the cartel figures out that they've been hijacked. By then we'll be long gone. And maybe they'll have figured out that Nadia and Zander were conned."

"They might still kill them."

"They might. But with the FBI in the picture, would they want to risk killing people they know were duped?"

"Zander and Nadia chose this life, even if they aren't good at it."

"You're right, they did," Danny said. "And that's why they're fair game. But I sure don't think they deserve to die."

"You're sweet on her."

"You jealous?"

"Just saying."

"Hustling her has been way too easy. She's not really a criminal. If I can keep her from being killed, I will."

Genie squeezed his hand. "Just as long as we can get away clean."

"We will."

"There are a lot of moving parts in this scam. Those diamonds better be there."

"They'll be there. We'll take them and we'll disappear."

LATER THAT EVENING, Lang stopped in at Clyde's Place. It was quiet, even for a Sunday night. There were three men at the bar, and another six people sitting at tables. Johnston waved at him from a table near the jukebox. MacBurn was sitting with him.

Lang walked over to their table, but he didn't sit down.

"I thought you might come in here," Johnston said.

Lang shook his head. "You're a real horse's ass."

"I apologize. I really do. I know I was drunk. This morning, my cousin told me what I said. I should have kept my mouth shut."

"Sit down," MacBurn said. "Have a beer."

Land looked from one to the other and then pulled out a chair. "You scared my wife."

"I'm sorry."

"She heard noises all night. Thought somebody was sneaking around in the yard."

"But no one was there?" MacBurn asked.

"No, just took her a long time to settle down."

"She at home now?"

"Naw, took her to the airport. She's got work tomorrow."

"Well, that's a shame. Hope she decides to stay."

"That probably depends on if I can get the farm back up."

"Hard to do," MacBurn said.

"That's for sure," Johnston added. "Let me get us some beers." He went up to the bar.

MacBurn continued. "What happened to that post office job?"

"Didn't happen."

"You should talk to some of the other guys. They might still be hiring at the new fulfillment center."

"Thought I'd wait until after our little project was done."

"Sure."

Johnston came back with three cans of beer.

"Speaking of our little project..." MacBurn glanced around to make sure no one was sitting within earshot. "I've been thinking about the three guys we need to help drive."

Johnston nodded. "Need to be guys in our club."

"Yeah," MacBurn said. "But they need to be guys who don't ask questions and know how to keep their mouths shut. Word can't leak out. Not even to our own people. Some of them are a little jittery about action. Somebody gets arrested, they can't tell the cops what they don't know."

"What about Darrel and his cousins?" Johnston asked.

"I don't really know them," Lang said.

"Darrel's the one with the tattoo on his neck. They were in prison together. Car theft ring. They don't look like much, but they won't talk, and prison doesn't scare them."

"I know who you're talking about," MacBurn said. "Let's corral them after next week's meet-up. Take their temperature."

They made small talk until they finished their beers. "I've got to go," Lang said.

"What's your hurry?"

"Need to make an early start."

"I really am sorry about yesterday," Johnston said.

"Just don't do it next time," Lang replied.

After Lang left the bar, Johnston said, "I really wasn't all that drunk."

MacBurn looked at him quizzically.

"I didn't believe that woman was his wife."

"So you were jerking him around?"

Johnston nodded.

"We need him," MacBurn said. "He's proven he's rock solid."

"Yeah, well, I snuck out there—"

"To the farm?"

"Yeah. And they were in bed together."

MacBurn shook his head in disbelief. "And you saw them screwing?"

"I didn't look that hard—it was dark, okay, but, yeah, that's what they were doing."

"Christ, Ray, do you believe him now?"

"On his family life? I don't know. I will say that I believe him enough to trust him with our project."

MONDAY MORNING, Special Agent-in-Charge Vincent was on a secure video call with the Counterterrorism Task Force liaisons from ICE, ATF, and the National Defense Agency. "So that's where we're at. We've got less than two weeks."

"So you'll need control of the port?" Sanderson, the ICE liaison asked.

"Have you still got an ongoing investigation?"

Sanderson turned to someone behind him for a moment. "Yes, Customs has an investigation underway."

"I assume they have surveillance already set up. Can we piggy-back on their operation? We don't want our people tripping all over each other."

"We've got you covered."

Gregory from ATF said, "Agent Osborne—you've worked with him in the past, I think?"

"Yes, I have."

"He's working the C-4 angle."

"Excellent."

"And we'll continue to gather intel from our overseas assets," Garcia said. "Khan has dropped off our radar, but we're working all our contacts."

A WEEK LATER, on a Tuesday night, Ray Johnston and an old army buddy drove up to a closed auto shop in an industrial section of Kansas City. They were driving a stolen Ford Focus. "You sure this guy can be trusted?" Johnston asked.

"I watched him burn down a nigger's house. This guy hates them."

They pulled up into the driveway. The garage door rolled up, and they drove inside. A long workbench with rows of tool drawers underneath ran across the back of the work space. A big man with a long beard and tattoos on his hands stood to one side. He lowered the garage door. Johnston and his army buddy got out of the car. "Hey, Buster," the army buddy said.

"It's been a long time." The big man had a pistol holstered at his hip. "I've got to frisk you. Nothing personal. My freedom is more important to me than any notions of trust that you think I should have."

"Knock yourself out," Johnston said. He held his arms out.

The big man ran his hands over him methodically. "All done."

Then he frisked the army buddy. "Glad that's over with. Let's get down to business."

He walked them over to a work bench and opened a box that contained six bricks of C-4.

"Look like blocks of clay," the army buddy said.

"Except they blow up," Johnston replied.

"You know what to do with them?" the big man asked.

"You bet."

"Got my cash?"

"Yep." Johnston went back to the car and brought back a plastic grocery bag.

The big man looked inside. "Is it all here?"

"Yes, sir," Johnston said.

The big man counted the money out onto the table. "We won't ever see each other again."

"If you say so."

"I know so."

Johnston picked up the box and carried it back to the trunk of the Ford. The big man pressed the controller to raise the garage door. Johnston and his army buddy drove away.

THE BIG MAN with the long beard locked the doors to the auto shop and went into the back room. He turned on the laptop computer sitting on the steel desk and watched the surveillance footage of his transaction with Johnston. Then he got out his phone. "Vincent? It's Osborne. The job's done. I sold them the fake C-4. They didn't even blink."

"You put the special additive in the binder?"

"Yeah, you'll be able to identify those exact blocks."

"And you're sure that stuff isn't volatile?"

"Looks like C-4, feels like C-4, but it will not blow up. Now the blasting caps, that's another matter."

"I understand. Thanks for your help."

"You bet. I'm sending you the surveillance footage now; you'll get my final report tomorrow." He emailed the file to Vincent.

"Got it."

"Anything else?"

"No, we're done at your end."

Osborne closed his laptop and left through the backdoor into the alley.

DANNY AND NADIA lay together in a Holiday Inn Express, her head on his shoulder, the sheets half off the bed, the lamp on her night table lighting up half her pillow and leaving most of the room in shadow. "We've had a great run," Danny said, putting on his concerned voice. "But now things are going to change."

She leaned up on her elbow. "What do you mean?"

"The container is due next week. The FBI is going to scoop up that package. Best case one: They get the package without tipping off anyone. It doesn't contain anything they're really interested it. They give it back to you, you pass it to the courier, they follow the courier just to keep their hand in the game, arrest him somewhere down the line, Tehrani never finds out, but he can't use you anymore."

"Sounds wonderful," she said. "I'll be glad when it's over."

"Best case two: Same as above, but the package is exactly what they want. They substitute something else and start trailing the substitution. They want you to stay in contact with Tehrani and to keep providing information for their ongoing investigation."

"I see what you're saying. Tehrani could find out we're helping the FBI and our family could be in danger in Iran. That's best case scenario two? That's not a good outcome at all."

"And what if we're not talking best case? What if the terrorists find out about the FBI? What if there's a gunfight at your warehouse? How long before Tehrani suspects you? How long before Tehrani's friends come to kill you just to be sure?"

"That's not going to happen," Nadia said. "The FBI isn't going to let that happen."

"I hope you're right. But sometimes it's not about competence. Sometimes it's just the luck of the draw. So you've got to have two plans. One with the FBI and one without."

"We can't run," she said. "Our lives are here. Our business is here."

He took her hand. "Sometimes you have to do what you don't want to do if you want to save your life."

"Zander would never agree."

"He'll agree if it's the only way to save his family."

She shook her head.

"Look, you might just need to hide out temporarily. What's a few days or a few months compared to the rest of your life? Promise me you'll think about it."

"Okay," she said, "I'll think about it, but I don't think it's really necessary."

"Thank you." He rubbed her shoulder, and then he kissed her.

"Now it's my turn," Nadia said. "What about you and Genie? As soon as the FBI has the package, won't they arrest you?"

"They promised us a pass on the port jobs, same as you, so we'll be fine."

"You're going to stay?"

"As far as I know, we're not going anywhere."

"The cartel is probably watching you."

"We know. They connected Genie to our port guy. Just means we need to be extra careful not to step on their toes."

"I'm so glad you're going to stay."

"You need to be safe. That's the most important thing."

TWO DAYS LATER, after the Fatherland Volk meet-up at the rifle range at the Jacobs's farm just south of Summerville, MacBurn, Johnston, and Lang stood in the muddy grass parking by the gravel road, watching everyone leave.

"Hey, Darrel," Johnston said.

A small, thin man with a weathered face and scraggly beard turned his head.

"You got a minute?"

Darrel and two other guys, very similar in appearance, meandered over, their rifles under their arms. "What's up, Ray?"

"Hey, fellas," MacBurn said. "Been glad to see you guys come out to the activities. Some of the guys treat the club as a social thing, but you guys get it."

Darrel and his cousins glanced at each other. "Got to stay prepared."

"You guys work at the new fulfillment center?"

"Driving forklifts."

"You guys still on parole?"

"You got something in mind?"

"You know Lang?"

"Seen him around."

"He's living out at his grandpa's place."

Darrel shifted for one foot to the other. "This conversation going somewhere?"

Johnston cut in. "We've got a special project. It's the kind of project that's going to make a big difference."

"If you're talking about burning out some cross-breeders, count us in," Darrel replied.

"Bigger than that, lots bigger. Going to be national news."

"What have you got in mind?"

"We need three guys with us, three guys who won't flinch, three guys who can keep their mouths shut. If you don't want in, that's fine, we understand. Everyone's got to make their own decision, and we'll see you at the next meet-up. But if you're those guys, if you do want to make a big impact, you give me a call tomorrow, and we'll fill you in."

Darrel nodded.

"You give me a call, either way."

"I will."

"You fellas have a nice evening."

They watched Darrel and his cousins get into a Silverado truck.

"You think they're in?" Lang asked.

"They're in," Johnston said.

"We'll find out tomorrow," MacBurn replied.

BACK IN POINT JERICHO, Danny and Genie walked into Martinez's office at the plastics extrusion plant and sat down in the chairs facing his desk. Martinez looked up from some paperwork. "Why are you here?"

"We've done what you asked," Danny said.

"More than our original deal," Genie added.

"So it's time for you to cut us loose."

Martinez shook his head. "When we've got the package in hand, then your part is done. Not a moment before. Until then, you'll do whatever I ask."

"I'm going to talk to Garcia," Danny said.

"Talk to whoever you want. This is a Joint Task Force operation. Victor is in charge, and I work for him."

"Martinez, the front end of this job is in the bag."

"Don't care. I won't know what I need until we're all done."

"What about Zander and Nadia? Have you made a plan for them?"

"You've started caring about her since you've been sleeping with her?"

"They're US citizens. You can't just leave them out in the wind."

"They're not going to have any trouble."

"You're going to take this special package—whatever that is—and the terrorists aren't going to torture and murder them just to be sure? That'll look great in the report."

"I said they're not going to have any trouble."

"You need to scoop them up and hide them away. How hard is that?"

"You two need to worry about your own problems. As soon as this operation is done, our deal is over, and it's going to be my pleasure to hunt you down, lock you up, and throw away the key."

"You're certainly making yourself clear."

"I hope I am."

Danny and Genie strolled out through the empty warehouse and got back in Danny's Cadillac. The sun cut through the clouds in the west. Danny put on his sunglasses.

"You sold him," Genie said. "He's going to move them."

"I hope so."

"Definitely sold him. You know these Feds. They talk a hard game, but they've all got drawers of Boy Scout merit badges back at their moms' houses."

"The honest ones do."

"They all do. It's just that the honest ones know which drawers they're in."

LATER THAT EVENING, Danny and Nadia were sitting in a booth in a pizza restaurant in a strip mall next to a movie multiplex, a half-finished pizza and a pitcher of beer on the table between them. "I'm surprised the pizza is this good," Danny said.

"You're surprised when any restaurant in this town is any good," Nadia replied.

"Guilty as charged." He took a sip from his beer glass. "Change of subject."

"That sounds ominous."

"I don't want to nag—"

"Then don't. Let's just enjoy this time together."

"Let me say what I have to say. Have you talked with Zander about making an escape plan?"

"Not yet."

"You can't leave this to chance. You have to have a plan."

"We'll be fine."

"I worry about you."

"I know. And it's sweet. But you've got nothing to worry about."

"If things go ass-up, I won't be able to help. Genie and I will be in the wind."

"Then things better not go wrong. I don't want you to leave."

"And I don't want to leave."

"So we can quit talking about this."

"Okay."

She smiled. "And you can start telling me how much you love me."

THE NEXT MORNING, when Danny got back to their rental, he found Genie sitting in the kitchen drinking coffee and reading the newspaper on her smartphone. "How'd it go?" she asked. She set her phone down on the table.

He poured a cup of coffee and sat down beside her. "Everything is fine. You know I've been after her to make an escape plan in case the terrorist thing blows up?"

"Yeah."

"She's not going to do it."

"Really? That doesn't make sense," Genie said.

"She's avoiding the subject."

"Which is crazy."

"Unless the diamonds are definitely, absolutely in this shipment."

Genie chuckled. "Because then, no matter what, they can't leave. They have to deliver the diamonds, because having terrorists after you is not even half as bad as having terrorists and the Orange Hill Cartel after you."

"Exactly."

"Good news for us."

"And bad news for them," he replied. "Their lives are going to get a lot more complicated."

"You tried to warn her. Begged her to makes her own escape plan. Besides, the FBI is going to collect them."

"We can't be sure of that."

"Honey, you sold Martinez on putting them into protective custody. He needs them for his case, even if he doesn't care if they live or die. He's going to get them out of our way. It's going to happen."

"I hope you're right. There's nothing more I can do to help her."

AFTER LUNCH, while Lang was attaching a bush hog to his tractor so he could cut brush along the right-of-way ditches on the west side of the farm, he got a call from MacBurn. "Ray heard from Darrel. They're in."

"We all going to meet?"

"He's going to get them up to speed. There's no reason for us to be seen with them. All their communication will be through him. They won't find out about the barn until it's time to drive away."

"That's smart."

"Start working on your alibi."

"I'll be ready."

"Won't be long now."

"Have you heard something?"

"Not yet. I've just got a feeling."

MacBurn ended the call. Lang went into the farmhouse and made a call to Victor from an encrypted link on his computer.

"Special Agent Victor's phone."

"I need to talk."

"One moment."

He waited on the line, looking out the window into the yard as if he'd be able to tell if someone were coming. Finally Victor answered. "Yeah?"

"We've got the other drivers. And the C-4."

"I know about the C-4. It's fake. Looks and feels like the real thing, but it won't explode."

"MacBurn thinks we'll have the uranium real soon."

"He have a definite date?"

"No, not yet."

"So you're back in tight?"

"Yes."

"Did you sleep with your fake wife?"

Lang hesitated. "Yes. Yes, I did."

"But you didn't tell her anything?"

"No, sir."

"I've got a hard question for you."

"Shoot."

"Do you want to stay in after the sting?"

"After we take down this cell?"

"Yes. I know you've been under almost a year, but this might be our best opportunity to infiltrate more cells of the Fatherland Volk."

"So I'd be arrested with the others?"

"Yeah, you'd go to jail with the rest of them. It would look too suspicious if you managed to escape. We'll rig up some way to get you out on bail, and you'd stay undercover."

"I'd have to think about it."

"You do that."

9
___

SHOWTIME

Just after 3:00 a.m., the Southern Lights cargo ship docked at the Port of Point Jericho. By 5:30 the Hashemis' container had been loaded on a truck chassis. Customs agents had the process under video surveillance from their command center in a shack near the port exit. An FBI agent had been substituted for the Hashemis' usual semitruck driver. The sun was coming up over the ocean as he drove the container out of the port, into the nearby warehouse district, and up to the loading dock behind the Hashemi building.

The Hashemi Carpets & Arts parking lot looked exactly as it should. Four cars were parked at the far end of the lot to represent the four warehouse workers who would normally be here to unload a container. Zander's and Nadia's cars were parked in front, by the main entrance. But inside the warehouse, Martinez and three other FBI agents, dressed like warehouse workers, were waiting with Zander and Nadia for the container to be backed up to the loading dock, while another agent sat in the offices at a computer, monitoring the drone surveillance of the immediate area, and two more agents lay hidden in the back of one of the parked cars.

When Zander heard the semitruck backing up to the loading

dock, he opened the warehouse doors and watched the truck come to a stop. The FBI truck driver climbed down from the cab and walked past him into the warehouse.

"Anything strange?" Martinez asked.

"I didn't see anyone," the truck driver said.

Zander turned to Martinez. "Okay, we know how to do this. Just stay out of the way, and we'll get this done as quickly as possible."

Martinez radioed the agent monitoring the drones. "Have we got complete control of the perimeter?"

"We own the two blocks around this building."

Martinez turned to Zander and Nadia. "Go ahead."

Zander and Nadia pulled open the doors on the back of the container. Inside, pallets were stacked with carpets that had been folded into thirds and then rolled up and wrapped in Tyvek wrap. Heavy netting covered the stacked carpets to hold them on the pallet. Zander used a forklift to move the first pallet into the warehouse. He and Nadia couldn't make any mistakes now. They had to find the special package without finding the diamonds. Their lives depended on it.

Nadia walked around the stacked pallet, studying the outer surfaces, looking for anything out of the ordinary. "Not here."

Zander moved another pallet into the warehouse, setting it down next to the first. Nadia walked around this one, stooped and examined the edge of the Tyvek on one carpet, and shook her head.

Zander moved the third pallet in. Nadia walked around to the left, stopped, and pulled at a Tyvek wrapper in the middle of the stack that was a different color from the others. "Think I found it."

She dragged over a stepladder and climbed up to the top to unhook the netting holding the carpet stack in place. "Give me some help here. We need to get this one out." She pointed to the carpet with the different colored wrapper. "Be careful with the other carpets. They're valuable." The FBI agents lifted the carpets above it down onto the closest worktable, laying them out in a row. Nadia put her hand on the differently colored wrapper. "Great. Now put this one on the floor over there." She pointed to an open area away from the pallet.

Two agents hefted the rolled carpet off the pallet and carried it over to the spot she'd indicated. Nadia got down on her hands and knees to unwrap the Tyvek. She didn't know what she'd found, but she knew it wasn't the diamonds. The carpet with the diamonds inside was always wrapped with the same color of wrapper as the rest of the carpets. After she removed the wrapper, she saw that a plug of fabric was pushed into each end of the roll. When she pulled out one plug, she could see a package at the center of the roll. She unrolled the carpet. A rectangular box wrapped in brown craft paper and sealed with clear package tape was left sitting on what was obviously a cheap, machine-made carpet.

"This is the package?" Martinez asked.

"That's how we find them," Nadia said.

"Test it," Martinez said. The two agents carried the package to the farthest worktable. Agent Ables got out a Geiger counter.

Zander climbed down from the forklift. "What's that?"

"Checking for radiation," Ables said.

"Radiation? And you didn't warn us?"

She ran the Geiger counter's wand over the package. "There's something," she said, "but not much. Can't be natural or enriched uranium."

"So the carpets are safe?" Zander asked.

"Yes."

"Open the package," Martinez said.

Ables and one of the other agents put on coveralls with hooded masks and protective gloves before they unwrapped the package. Inside was a white plastic box. Ables held the Geiger counter wand up close to the box while the other agent inched off the top. Inside was a plastic bag full of a yellowish power. "Depleted uranium," Ables said.

"That's all?" Martinez asked.

"Yes."

"So the terrorists are just shining them on."

"Looks like it, sir. You'd have to inhale this stuff for it to be dangerous."

"What are you talking about?" Nadia asked.

"Nothing that concerns you," Martinez said. He turned back to Ables. "Place the marker in the package, and close it up."

The agents replaced the top, and then rewrapped and taped the box. Martinez inspected the results. "Perfect."

Martinez turned to Zander. "What would you do now?"

"Just like we told you. Go about our normal business and wait for the courier. A guy should come by in the next few hours."

"Always a guy?"

"Always a guy dressed like a regular American."

"So now we wait."

"Yes. If you don't mind, we're going to inventory the carpets."

"That's what you'd normally do?"

"Yes."

"Then go ahead."

The FBI agents disappeared into the offices. Zander and Nadia grinned at each other. Their plan had worked. Now all they had to do was wait out the FBI and then find the diamonds for Mr. Wishes.

Zander used the forklift to bring the last pallet of carpets into the warehouse. Then he and Nadia inventoried the carpets that were on the worktable, Zander calling out the tag numbers and Nadia checking them against the invoice numbers on a spreadsheet on her tablet. Then they inspected each carpet, unrolling it and verifying its authenticity before rerolling it and lugging it to the shelves. When they finished with the carpets that were already on the bench, they started working through the carpets on the pallets. "I'm not used to this heavy work," Nadia said. "I wish we had our guys to help us."

"I know," Zander said. His shirt was stained with sweat.

Shortly after 10:00 a.m., a clean-shaven man with wavy brown hair, wearing dark blue jeans and a leather jacket, came into the warehouse through the loading dock. He held up one hand. "Mr. Hashemi. Please forgive the intrusion."

Zander stood up from the carpet he was examining, while Nadia turned away. "I'm sorry, my friend, we're not a retail store. Only wholesale. I can suggest a local retailer."

"I'm a friend of a friend," the man said. "You received a package for me."

Zander extended his hand. "Peace be upon you."

The man shook it. "And also on you."

Zander pointed toward the wrapped package on the far work-table. "There it is."

The man looked at the package as if he recognized it. "Thanks for your trouble."

"It was nothing."

The man left. Zander walked to the loading dock door and watched him get into a tan Camry and drive away.

Martinez and two of the agents hurried into the warehouse from the offices. "Good work," he said.

"I'm glad that's over with," Nadia replied.

"It's not over yet. This is just the beginning."

"What do you mean?" Zander asked. "They've got the package, and you're on them."

"But if anything goes wrong before we arrest them, they might decide you tipped us off."

"We'll take that chance," Zander said.

"Don't argue. We're taking you into protective custody. It'll look like you've been arrested, and that will give you a cover story."

"You never told us anything about this," Nadia said.

"We can't risk you being harmed. It will probably only be for twenty-four to forty-eight hours." He turned to Ables, who had just entered the room. "Did you get a tracker on the Camry?"

"Yes, sir. We've got a tracker on it, and a drone over it. Rafe and Sally are in pursuit."

"Let's wrap this up here." He turned back to Zander and Nadia. "Time to go."

"What about my wife? My daughter?" Zander asked. "I can't leave them."

"Agents are at your house right now."

"Boss," Ables said, "should I send two agents to pick up Briggs and Pullman?"

"We can't spare anyone right now. They'll have to wait."

"And we're leaving this building as is?"

"We can spare a drone, but that's all."

"What about local police?"

"I don't want them involved in this part. Can't risk word leaking out."

"But the drone that's here only has a couple of hours of battery left, and that's if it stays stationary."

"It'll have to do. Our priority is the terrorists. Once we have them in custody, we'll reevaluate."

DANNY AND GENIE were hiding in a stolen white plumber's van on the street just outside the entrance to the industrial park where they could keep an eye on the comings and goings from Hashemi Carpets & Arts. They'd been sitting there all night so that they could avoid any surveillance that the FBI would put in place just before the sting. They were dressed in jeans and boots, just like the Hashemis' warehouse workers, and they wore hooded sweatshirts, ballcaps, and gloves. As the day got brighter, they'd watched the semitruck carrying the container roll in, they'd watched the tan Camry come and go, and now they saw the Hashemis go by in the back seat of a Subaru driven by Agent Ables, followed by two other cars.

"See? Told you that you sold Martinez on collecting them," Genie said.

"If their luck holds out, they could do all right." Danny shook his Caffeination coffee to-go cup to confirm it was empty. "You ready?"

Genie watched the Subaru disappear around the corner. "Let's give it another minute."

Five minutes later, they drove down to the Hashemi building. Zander's and Nadia's cars were parked in front. No one was parked in the back. So far so good. They parked in the alley beside the Hashemi building, pulled up the hoods on their sweatshirts to avoid being

identified on the surveillance camera, and went in through a bathroom window that didn't have an alarm sensor. Genie was carrying a
small backpack. They crept down the hallway in the dark, looking in
the offices, using their phone flashlights to check for alarm sensors
on the interior doors. The building was empty. Genie pushed open
the door to the warehouse and turned on the lights. Four pallets of
rolled carpets sat in the open, one pallet almost empty. Three rolled
carpets sat on a worktable. One carpet lay unrolled on the concrete
floor.

"The FBI left this place unprotected," Genie said.

"Manpower shortage or just in a big fat hurry? Gone for good or
coming back?"

"This is going to be a lot of work."

"Then we've got to work smart. Let's think it through," Danny
replied.

"They didn't want the FBI to find the diamonds."

"If there was a pattern to how the terrorist packages were loaded
in the past, Zander and Nadia would know what it is."

"And after they found the special package, they wouldn't have
been looking for the diamonds with the FBI around," Genie said.

"So the short pallet and the rolled carpets on the table are probably out. What did the computer info tell us?"

"Mumbai was the point of origin."

"And that's where the India Diamond Trading Centre is," Danny
continued.

"So the diamonds could be in the first pallet that was loaded."

"But all the pallets were loaded there."

"True. Any other clues?" Genie asked.

"How would they know where the special package was?"

"All the carpets are folded, rolled, and wrapped."

"What about the wrappers?"

Danny looked at the shelves. "All the shelved carpets are
wrapped."

"What about this carpet over here?" She pointed to a carpet that
was lying to the side, unrolled, but still folded.

Danny knelt beside it and ran his hand across the surface. "This is not an expensive rug, even I can tell that."

"Where's its wrapper?"

"Right here." Danny picked up one end of the wrapper. "It's a different color from the other wrappers."

"Now we have a clue."

They went back to the pallets, starting with the one that was closest to the loading dock and most likely the last off/first on the container. They scanned each side of the stack of carpets, looking for any differences in the color of the wrapper. Nothing. They went to the next pallet and repeated the process. Every wrapper seemed to be exactly the same.

"What are we missing?" Danny asked.

They went to the last full pallet, working around the sides of the stack methodically, but there were no differences in the wrappers.

"Okay," Danny said. "What more do we know?"

"Nadia updated the computer records, indicating that this shipment was special. That was before they found out about the terrorist package."

"We know the cartel diamonds are supposed to come in during this time frame. That was solid intel. That's what brought us here."

"And we know that Nadia and Zander weren't willing to run."

"The diamonds are here."

"We could unwrap all the carpets."

"We will if we have to."

Danny walked around the stacks of carpets. "We've got to think like the cartel."

"We wouldn't want anyone to be able to find the diamonds."

"But we wouldn't want them to be too hard to get our hands on."

"Or too easy," Genie continued. "We're talking ten million dollars in diamonds. If someone broke into the container in transit, they would steal from the pallet closest to the door. They wouldn't know about the diamonds, they'd be after carpets. Likewise at the dock."

"So let's focus on the stack that came from the back of the container."

Danny carried the stepladder over to the pallet, climbed to the top, and unhooked the netting holding the stack in place. Then he pushed a rolled carpet off the top of the stack. Genie knelt to unwrap it and unroll it. Nothing inside. He pushed another carpet off the stack. Genie unwrapped it and unrolled it. Nothing. They continued working their way down the stack. Soon Danny was on his feet, and they were both pushing carpets off the stack and unwrapping them and unrolling them, the still-folded carpets piling up around the diminishing stack.

Finally, on the second to the last layer of carpets, Danny pulled the middle carpet out, unwrapped it and unrolled it. At the inside edge, a bit of black fabric stuck out from inside the folded carpet. "Genie, give me a hand."

She looked at him quizzically.

"Let's drag it over to the open area where we can unfold it."

They each took an end and dragged it away from the pallets. Then they got down on their hands and knees and unfolded the carpet. A narrow black tube was taped along one end. Danny pulled a lockback knife from his pocket and slit the length of the tube, exposing a glittering field of diamonds. "Oh baby," he said.

Genie laughed. "Makes you horny just looking at them, doesn't it?"

"No time to lose."

Genie took a zippered bag from her backpack. She scooped the diamonds into the bag, making sure to get the last few out of the corners of the tube. "How much do you think?"

"I think Billy wasn't lying. Got to be ten million."

"So at least one hundred thousand our end."

"At least."

They left the building the same way they came in. There was no one in the alley outside the bathroom. As they were getting back into the plumber's van, Genie heard a faint buzzing as the breeze shifted. "Quiet," she said. "Can you hear that?"

They stood with their gloved hands on the van doors, listening for anything unusual. The breeze fluttered. "There it is," Genie said. "Did you hear it?"

Danny glanced up quickly. "Christ. It's a drone. Straight above us."

They jumped into the van and sped out of the alley, Danny behind the wheel. The front parking lot was empty except for Zander's and Nadia's cars. "Anyone on the street?" Danny asked.

"No one I can see."

"Is the drone following us?"

"I can't tell."

He drove west on Chance Martin Drive, heading toward the suburbs, staying just above the speed limit, and circled around through a neighborhood of two-story brick homes. The drone was still above them. "The cops got to be on their way."

"Then we've got to stay ahead of them."

Danny turned on a cross street and headed north, Genie scrutinizing their surrounding for possible law enforcement, until he pulled into a Walmart and parked the van in the far corner of the parking lot. Then they walked across the street into a residential neighborhood of duplexes and single-family houses and found the stolen Subaru just where they had left it. There were no surveillance cameras, no dog walkers, no children playing, but the drone was still above them.

They climbed into the Subaru and drove downtown to the parking garage where they had left their Cadillac, complete with their go bag, new IDs, and credit cards, on the third level. They pulled in beside it and switched vehicles.

"Now's the tricky part," Danny said.

They took off their sweatshirts and caps and tossed them into the back seat. Then they moved to a parking space near the exit and waited. There were no sirens, no flashing lights, no police officers rushing the parking ramp with guns drawn. A minivan drove out of the ramp. They fell in behind it, exited the ramp, and cruised down Martin Luther King Drive. "Take a look?" Genie asked.

Danny nodded. She lowered her window and stuck her head out. The sky was clear. "We've lost it."

"You sure?"

She took another look. "Yeah. It's gone."

They took the closest exit onto the beltway and drove south to the first interstate rest stop, where they pulled up in front of the welcome center. "You know," Danny said, "I like most technology. It can be a pain in the ass to learn, but it's usually helpful. But I hate drones."

"Preaching to the choir, baby."

They went into the welcome center, changed clothes in the restrooms, and put their old clothes into an outside trashcan.

"We're almost in the clear," Genie said.

"Almost," Danny replied. "Pull up your map app and route us to Cincinnati."

MEANWHILE, the drone operator who'd been guiding the drone over the Hashemi building was on the phone with Martinez. "I've had a hell of a time getting ahold of you."

"Kind of busy right now. What's up?"

"Two people entered the Hashemi building. They were in there about an hour. When they came out I got their images and their license plate number."

"Why is this so important? Were they carrying anything?"

"No, but I just ran the images. They matched Briggs and Pullman. Thought you would want to know."

"Are you tracking them?"

"I was, but I lost them in a parking garage downtown. Ran out of juice before I could find them again."

"Damn it. Arresting them would have been a nice bonus. Give those images and the license plate numbers to the local police. Don't say anything about the warehouse. Maybe they'll be able to catch them before they disappear."

. . .

LATER THAT AFTERNOON, Mr. Wishes parked next to the loading dock behind Hashemi Carpets & Arts. He'd called Zander several times since the container had been delivered, but no one had answered the phone. It was puzzling. He knew the Hashemis were too afraid to cross him after what had happened to Pauly Wright. They were pliable, easy to intimidate. He pulled on the loading dock door. Locked. He rang the bell. No one answered. He pounded on the door. Nothing. He picked the lock and flipped on the light switch. What had happened here? Four pallets of rolled carpets sat in the middle of the warehouse. They had to be this morning's shipment. But one of the pallets was mostly empty, and another had unwrapped but still folded carpets strewn haphazardly around it. Then he noticed two carpets laid out just beyond the pallets, one still folded in thirds and one completely unfolded. As he walked toward them, he saw the black diamond bag taped to one end of the unfolded carpet. It was slashed. He knelt down, felt inside the bag, it was empty. This didn't add up.

What had Zander told him? Two packages hidden in the load. Had the FBI stumbled over the diamonds searching for the other package? Doubtful. They wouldn't have slashed the bag. They would have taken their time, documented everything, peeled off the tape to keep all the evidence intact. And Zander and his sister would have taken precautions. They would have done everything they could to keep the Feds from finding the diamonds. And they wouldn't have taken the diamonds themselves. They just wouldn't. Their entire lives were here, and there was nowhere they could run where they couldn't be found.

He got out his phone. "Mitch? Start searching for the Hashemis. I want the wife and kid, and Zander and his sister. Find them. Take them. Don't hurt them unless you have to."

He walked back out onto the loading dock and down the steps to his car. Then he made another call. "It's me. Our goods are gone. I'm on it."

· · ·

AT SIX O'CLOCK, Nadia, Zander, Bonnie, and Tracy were in a conference room at the county jail. Several bags of Taco John's were open on the Formica table. Half-eaten burritos and tacos sat on their wrappers near partially consumed takeout cups of soft drinks. The monitor hanging from the back wall was showing a cable news channel. Tracy was coloring in a coloring book. Nadia was sitting at the far end of the table near the door. Zander stood on one side of the table with his arms crossed, while Bonnie paced back and forth on the other side, her shoes clicking on the tile floor with every step.

"This still doesn't make sense," Bonnie said.

"Relax," Zander said. "We're helping the FBI. We'll be out of here soon."

"Do you believe that, Nadia?"

Nadia shook her head. "I don't know."

"I just don't understand," Bonnie continued. "Why are we here? Tell me the truth."

Nadia listened to her brother trying to tell his wife as little as possible about what they'd done and at the same time not say anything that would upset Tracy. Finally, she cut in, "You remember Uncle had been arrested?"

"Yes," Bonnie said.

"Some people in the Iranian government were trying to make us do something wrong to let him go. So we told the FBI."

"The Iranian government?"

"Some people. We don't know if the Iranian government sanctioned it. That's for the FBI to figure out."

"What happened to your uncle?"

"He's okay," Zander said. "We found someone to help him."

Bonnie sat down at the conference table next to Tracy. "So the FBI brought us here—"

"To protect us," Nadia said. "We helped them spot the bad guys, and they're dealing with them right now."

"My God." Bonnie put her arms around her daughter.

"Yes. Now you understand."

"But we're safe," Zander said. "And we're going to stay safe."

Nadia put her elbows on the table, closed her eyes and rested her head in her hands. They were safe, but for how long? Mr. Wishes was definitely pissed off by now, unless he'd been to the warehouse and found the diamonds himself. At least the diamonds were still there. At least they'd warned him about this problem. Worst case, Mr. Wishes and his thugs would damage the carpets finding the diamonds, and she and Zander would have to take the loss. Not so bad.

But Tehrani was still out there. Would he believe they'd done their part? Would he think the FBI found out about the shipment from someone else? Would he believe the fake arrest? Maybe this protective custody was for the best. If he believed their arrest, they'd never have to smuggle anything for him again. But if he didn't believe it enough, Uncle and their cousins were certainly going to suffer.

Tears welled up in her eyes. And what about Danny? He'd been right. Everything was changing. Martinez had told Ables they couldn't spare the people to pick him up. So the FBI had reneged on their deal. Had he gotten away? Or were he and Genie locked in cells somewhere in this building? Would she and Zander be expected to testify against them? She palmed the tears out of her eyes. Well, she wouldn't do it. And she wouldn't let Zander do it, either.

10

CUT AND RUN

At 11:00 p.m., Omar Khan sat at a table in the kitchen of the left side of a duplex in Little Beirut, drinking hot tea. Everything was going to plan. MacBurn had been jubilant when he told him that they were ready to deliver the uranium. He probably wouldn't even notice that it was depleted, and if he did, so what? He'd still use it. He'd still blow up his targets. The uranium would still be traced back to the Middle East. The One World Jihad Union would still claim the credit. He'd have to find more uses for Tehrani. His smuggling route had run without the least bit of trouble.

He glanced up at Ibrahim, who stood watch at the kitchen window, an AR-15 rifle hanging from his shoulder. It was always handy to have a brother who looked European and spoke American English with only the tiniest accent. He'd proven himself on this trip. He'd leave him in charge of Hussain and Mohamed, send them to the Detroit cell to hide until he needed them again.

Tomorrow, they would all get fresh haircuts and new clothes. Just a group of proud American immigrants traveling for work. They would drive across the country, stopping only at places they'd vetted on other trips. In three days, they would meet MacBurn and hand over the uranium, then the others would head for Detroit, and he would cross back into Canada, pick up his rental car at the farm-house, fly out of Winnipeg, and be back with his family by the end of the week, God willing. And while the FBI scurried around, chasing after the racist fools, his operatives would find another weak point to exploit.

AGENT MARTINEZ, his drone operator, his computer specialist, and the local chief deputy sheriff sat in the back of an unmarked utility van on the street two block aways from Khan's duplex. The drone operator had the duplex under surveillance. No one had come in or out since the four men had arrived there that afternoon. In the mean-time, the computer specialist had used the stingray device to tap into Khan's phone. From there, she'd set up a Trojan horse via the weather app update. Now she was almost finished cloning the phone. Two other vehicles, each containing an FBI agent and a sheriff's depart-ment SWAT team, were in place north and south of the duplex.

Martinez was on his phone with Special Agent-in-Charge Victor. "We've got a recording of the call to the Fatherland Volk. And we tracked the origin, so we know it's the group Lang is on."

"You know where their meeting is?"

"Yes."

"And you know for a fact that Khan is in that house?" Victor asked.

"Yes, sir."

"Take them."

Martinez turned to the sheriff's chief deputy. "We've got the go-ahead."

"Boss," the computer specialist said, "I've finished cloning his phone. I'm processing the drive right now."

"Excellent work, Lorraine." Martinez turned to the drone opera-tor. "Any movement at the duplex?"

"Nothing."

Martinez put on his comms headset. "Sally? Rafe?"

"Yes, boss," they replied.

"It's a go."

Martinez and the chief deputy turned to the drone operator's screen and watched the two teams leave their SUVs and converge on the front and back of the duplex.

SALLY'S TEAM was at the front door. The lead SWAT officer raised a shotgun, blasted a breaching round through the front door lock, and jumped back behind the cover of the wall. "Federal Agents," Sally yelled. "On the ground now."

Automatic gunfire exploded through the windows. A second SWAT officer swung his body shield to one side, kicked in the door, swung his shield back in front of himself and pushed into the room. The first SWAT officer tossed the shotgun into the yard behind him and shouldered his Colt M4, firing short bursts around the second officer's body shield.

Inside the living room, two men, firing AR-15s, scampered back toward the kitchen, one of them taking cover behind an overstuffed chair.

Meanwhile, just as the shotgun blasted, Ibrahim rolled out the back door, Khan on his heels, and sprayed gunfire into the second SWAT team while they were setting up to take the door. The team fell back, and Khan and Ibrahim took cover behind a pair of steel trashcans.

The SWAT team spread out, firing on the trashcans to keep Ibrahim and Khan pinned down. Then Ibrahim jumped up from behind the trashcans, spraying them with automatic fire, while Khan ran. He turned the corner of the next house before Ibrahim fell. The closest SWAT officer kicked Ibrahim's rifle away and checked his pulse. "Dead."

"After the other one," Rafe yelled. Three SWAT officers ran toward the corner. The lead officer spoke into his comms. "Command. Where is he?"

"Looks like he's crouching between two cars parked on the next street," the drone operator replied.

The SWAT officers ran out onto the sidewalk around the corner. Neighbors, mainly Middle Eastern immigrants, were flooding out of their houses.

"What's going on?" someone yelled.

"Police," someone answered.

A group of neighbors, holding up their smartphones to videotape the interaction, surrounded the three SWAT officers. "Why are you here?" one of the neighbors asked.

"Sheriff's department. Go back in your houses," the lead SWAT officer said.

"Who are you harassing? You don't belong here."

The lead SWAT officer tapped his comms. "Command, we've got a lot of people on the street."

He heard the drone operator in his comms. "Your guy's mixed in with the crowd. I can't see him."

The three SWAT officers pushed through the crowd to the street. There was no one between or under the cars. They jogged away from the crowd, looking between the houses and the cars on the street, the neighbors following them. Nothing. "Command," the lead SWAT officer said, "the guy's gone."

"Go back to the duplex," Martinez said.

They jogged back to the duplex, shoving their way through the crowd gathering in the backyard. Rafe and two other SWAT officers were standing in the yard near the dead man.

The lead SWAT officer shook his head. "He got away."

"You report it in?" Rafe asked.

"Yeah."

"Help us set a perimeter for CSI."

The SWAT officers took up position between the neighbors and Ibrahim. "Stay back. This is an active crime scene."

"They murdered him," someone said.

"Probably planted the gun," someone else added.

"Stay back or you'll be arrested," one of the SWAT officers said.

Two sheriff's deputies carrying spotlights and police tape came around from the front yard.

Rafe went inside. Two Middle Eastern men were dead in the kitchen. Sally came down the hall from the bedrooms carrying a package. "We got it."

"One got away. I think it was Khan. And the neighbors are pissed."

Sally got on her comms. "We've got the package, boss, but one's loose. Rafe thinks he might be Khan."

"Keep the situation contained until CSI gets there," Martinez replied. "We'll get an all-points bulletin out on Khan."

Sally continued into the living room. One of the SWAT officers sat on the sofa with a tourniquet on his leg. Blood was leaking from his boot. Another SWAT officer had his arm in a sling.

"Where's the ambulance?" Sally asked.

"Minutes away," a third SWAT officer replied.

AFTER KHAN SAW the SWAT officers turn back, he crawled out from under the juniper bushes that were planted along the foundation of a Cape Cod two houses down the street and snuck away, staying as close to the sides of the houses as possible. At the first intersection, a four-way stop, he glanced back down the street toward the flashing blue lights before he hurried across the intersection to the cover of a ranch style house with no outside lights on. At the second intersection, he ran diagonally through the traffic light across the street to a Quick Trip. Two cars were parked in front of the building. A South Asian stood behind the counter, leaning on the cash register. Khan walked around to the parking lot behind the building, where he had left an old Chevrolet Impala parked next to the dumpster. The uranium was lost. His men taken or dead. The FBI must have been on to them from the very beginning. He knew the Fatherland Volk were amateurs, but this level of bungling—without a traitor inside the plan—was just not possible. Besides, they knew nothing about this part of the operation. Tehrani had to be the weak link. He must have trusted the wrong people. Or he'd told his superiors to save his own skin, and they'd told the Americans. Either way, he was a liability moving forward—

a liability that would have to be dealt with. Khan took his smart-phone from his pocket, pulled the chip, and snapped it in half. Then he tossed the phone into the dumpster. He drove off into the neighborhood, making random turns but always heading west, until he ended up on the boulevard that would take him to the freeway ramp.

He needed to get to the nearest unguarded border crossing to Canada. He wasn't going back through North Dakota. And he needed a new passport and driver's license. But first he needed a brother to provide transportation, so that there would be a gap in his journey that couldn't be traced. At the first interchange, he drove into a truck stop, parked on the far end of the lot, and went into the building to find a pay phone. There was an imam who could be trusted, a sleeper agent he'd never used before. What was his phone number? He took a list from his wallet, twenty numbers across and twenty numbers down, and hopscotched through them based on the pattern he'd memorized. He input the numbers.

"Hello?"

"Hello, my friend." He recited the password. "Can you help me?"

"Tell me what you need."

"I need someone to drive me from one location to another. Several hundred miles."

"I see."

"This person will make all the purchases—gas, food. He will be reimbursed, of course. And stop to rest only at certain freeway rest stops."

"So this person must be a man."

"No, a woman will do."

"Young? Old?"

"Discreet."

"Can you call me tomorrow?"

"From a different phone."

Khan bought a cheap cellphone on his way back to his car. He got his go-bag from the trunk and sat down in the driver's seat. Inside the bag were an envelope of cash, a pistol, and an electric razor. He adjusted the rearview mirror so that he could see himself, turned on the razor, and started shaving off his beard.

AT 11:30 P.M., Mr. Wishes, driving a Toyota Avalon, pulled into a parking spot across the street from the county jail. A small man dressed in a ballcap and a hoodie stepped out of the shadows and got into the passenger's side. "Okay, Mitch," Mr. Wishes said. "Start from the top."

Mitch pulled a scrap of paper from his pocket. "The Feds raided the warehouse this morning. They were set up at the dock when the container was unloaded."

"Our container? Our package?"

"Definitely our container. The Hashemis were arrested. Brought here."

"What does our inside guy say?"

"It's some terrorist task force beef. A sting on some terrorist group."

"But no mention of us or our package?"

"Nothing. Hashemis weren't even allowed a phone call."

"What about the wife and kid?"

"They got them all. Our guy says they're raiding another house this evening down in Little Beirut, so who knows when they'll be finished kicking down doors."

Mr. Wishes pointed his finger at Mitch's chest. "Two guys are going to be watching this place twenty-four seven. And I mean watching, not sleeping. The Hashemis don't leave here without me knowing about it. Anybody who screws up is going to answer to me."

"Who do you want me to put on this job?"

"That's your problem. Get out of my car."

Mr. Wishes watched Mitch climb into a Chevy Silverado. Christ. What kind of stupid had the Hashemis gotten themselves into? They had connections in Asia and Europe. That was what made them so useful. Until they weren't. And if all this police attention wasn't about the diamonds, did the cops have them? Or had the Hashemis hidden them away? Maybe the diamonds were still in the warehouse. Maybe the Hashemis hadn't used them as a bargaining chip. 'Cause they'd be too afraid to do that. They knew exactly what would happen if they screwed the cartel. Life in prison was better than that.

Mr. Wishes backed out of his parking space. Were the cops watching the warehouse? Was it worth the trouble of conducting a thorough search? If the cops had their hands full busting terrorists, maybe this was the best time. He got out his phone. "Cody?"

"Yeah, boss."

"Get two guys and meet me across the street from the Hashemis' warehouse. Chop-chop."

"I'm on it."

He took a right at the intersection. He had his bases covered. If the cartel was going to blame someone, it wasn't going to be him.

LANG WAS AWAKENED by the loud ping from his computer that indicated an incoming call. He rolled out of bed, input his password, and clicked on the phone app. "Yeah?"

He heard Victor's voice. "We've got the terrorists and the uranium. It's depleted, so we caught another break there."

Lang stifled a yawn. "When's the meet?"

"In two days at a rest stop on I 74 in Illinois."

"Finally."

"Martinez will coordinate with you on the arrests."

"Great."

"So, Joe, what's your decision about staying under?"

"I can't commit to forever, but I'll go in for the next phase, find out the who and where, then somebody else can take it over."

"Might take six months."

"I know."

"Good luck at the bust. I'll see you in an interrogation room afterward. We'll sort out the details then."

. . .

MARTINEZ LEANED BACK in his chair and rubbed his eyes. So far so good. They'd rolled up the jihadis, they had control of the depleted uranium, the C-4 was phony. They were on deck to take down the Fatherland Volk cell. Would have been better if they had a live jihadi, but so it goes.

Agent Ables, back in her civilian clothes, knocked on his open door. He sat up. "Well?"

She shook her head. "Briggs and Pullman did take something from the warehouse. Something that was hidden in a black bag rolled up in another carpet. Made a mess doing it. And they really are gone. They cleaned out their rental, and they aren't at any of their usual spots."

"That's a shame. I hate to leave them on the streets. Who was the union guy they were hooked up with at the port?"

"Stowe."

"Check with Customs. If it won't mess up their case, pull him in for a chat."

"Now?"

"Tomorrow. We all set for the Fatherland Volk?"

"Yes, sir. But we don't have enough bodies to keep anyone here."

"Doesn't matter. Was our marker in with the uranium?"

"Yes. It's definitely the same package."

"So we've got the physical evidence. There's no jihadis to prosecute. As long as we have Hashemi and Wright's testimony, we're set."

THE NEXT MORNING, two plainclothes customs agents brought Stowe to the county jail in handcuffs. They came in through the loading dock at the back and led him down an employee-only hallway to a small storeroom where Martinez was sitting behind a fold-up card table waiting for him. The customs agents put Stowe in the folding chair across from Martinez.

"Thanks, guys," Martinez said. "You can take off the cuffs."

The taller agent uncuffed Stowe. "We'll be in the break room."

Stowe rubbed his wrists. "What's this all about? Those guys

grabbed me at my house. Barely let me get dressed. Where's my lawyer?"

"Do you need a lawyer?" Martinez asked. "Have you committed a crime?"

"No."

"Do you want your union to know that you're being interviewed by the FBI?"

"You can't intimidate me."

"I don't have to intimidate you. I've got evidence—surveillance footage, photos, audio recordings of crimes being committed on the docks. Guess who's the leading man in this feature film?"

Stowe's face fell. "Then why I am back here instead of out front?"

"Because I'm not interested in you." He pulled a photo of Briggs and Pullman, taken in their front yard, out of a file folder and pushed it toward Stowe. "What can you tell me about these two?"

"I've seen that guy a couple of times. I don't know anything about him, not even his name."

"But you know he can drive a heavy rig?"

Stowe nodded.

"What about the woman?"

"This is off the record? No one will know I told you?"

"If you tell the truth."

"I thought she was my girlfriend—that we were just making a few bucks on the side."

"But?"

"She was using me. They had certain containers they wanted. When I told her I wanted out, she threatened me."

"With what?"

"Said the people they were working for would come after my family if I stopped helping them."

"When was that?"

"Over a month ago, easy."

"How many containers did you move for them after that?"

"None."

"None?"

"On the one hand, I was relieved; on the other hand, I was worried that she'd suddenly call out of the blue, wanting something crazy."

"And her name was?"

"Genie Pullman."

"And you haven't seen her at all? Not even for sex?"

"Not at all. Nothing. Period."

Martinez stood up. "Thank you for your time, Mr. Stowe. I'll tell the agents to take you home."

Martinez left via the loading dock. Briggs and Pullman must have taken something from the Hashemi building. Was that why they were in town to begin with? They'd used the terrorist sting to get Zander and Nadia out of the way, and then they'd swooped in. That's what the drone footage showed. Briggs had been manipulating Nadia just like Pullman had been manipulating Stowe. What did they take? Now that they were gone, he'd probably never find out. He got into his car and backed out of his parking space. But maybe they didn't get away. If Stowe was right and they were working for other people, maybe they'd been killed and dumped in the bay. Only time would tell. He'd have their information updated in the national database. That was all he could do.

THE FOLLOWING DAY, Bruce MacBurn and Ray Johnston sat in a stolen Dodge pickup truck facing out of a parking spot by a picnic table near the dog walking area of a rest stop on Interstate 74 in central Illinois. It was a beautiful, sunny afternoon, and they had the windows rolled down to take advantage of the breeze. They were drinking Cokes and watching for a red Matrix.

"There it is." Johnson gestured toward the Matrix that had just entered the rest stop. The Matrix pulled in beside them, placing them driver to driver. The Matrix's window lowered. The driver, a Middle Eastern man with a bushy mustache, looked up at MacBurn expectantly.

"Where's Khan?" MacBurn said.

The man spoke in accented English. "We can't always come and go as we please. I'm sure you understand."

Johnston leaned forward to see the man's face. "You got our package?"

"Yes, yes I do. It's in the back."

The three of them got out of their vehicles and gathered at the back of the Matrix. The man raised the liftback. "There you are."

A rectangular box wrapped in craft paper and mailing tape sat in the back. "Not very big," Johnston said.

MacBurn turned to the man. "Will this get the job done?"

"It will do exactly what you have in mind."

"And you can handle it?"

"The box? Yes. Wear gloves and masks when you work with the material inside."

MacBurn and Johnston stood looking at each other. "Jesus," Johnston said, picking up the box, "I don't know what you're worried about. You're not having any more kids."

He carried the box over to the pickup truck and put it behind the passenger's seat.

MacBurn turned back to the man. "Don't be looking for us. We're done with you guys."

The man smiled and nodded, got back in the Matrix, and drove away. Johnston got out the highway map. "Exit ramp is just three miles up the road."

"Let's get off there and drive the county roads for a couple of hours," MacBurn said. "Just in case."

"I'm with you."

MacBurn drove out of the rest stop. As they merged back onto the interstate, they glanced at each other and started laughing, slowly at first, and then louder, laughing so hard that their eyes watered.

"We did it," MacBurn said.

"Almost did it," Johnston said.

"Yep."

"Imagine what it's going to feel like when the vans explode."

"Fourth of July."

"Fourth of July is right. Independence Day. The start of our revolution."

"What did I tell you? Start some trouble, blame the monkeys, and our ranks will swell."

MARTINEZ SAT in the passenger's seat of a black Ford Explorer. His drone operator sat in the back, monitoring the drone on a laptop computer. "They took the package. We've got eyes on them. Rafe and Sally are a half mile behind."

Martinez texted Lang: *Your guys are in play.*

Lang replied: *Meeting at the barn tomorrow.*

Martinez called Ables. "Your team has the go-ahead. The meeting is at the barn at the farm tomorrow afternoon, so get set up, but stay well back. Don't want to spook them now."

"Don't worry, boss. We're on it. My team will take care of the principals at the barn, and Rafe and Sally will be ready to round up the rest of their club."

"And don't pull Lang out. Rough him up, arrest him, and process him with the others. We want to keep his cover intact."

BACK IN POINT JERICHO, Mr. Wishes got out of his car in the parking lot at Oceanside Park. The surf was rolling in hard, washing away the footprints of beach walkers, and the wind was damp and cold. Mitch was standing out on the sand, the hood of his hoodie up and his hands in his pants pockets.

Mr. Wishes turned up his collar of his jacket as he crossed the gravel. "What's up?"

"Nothing new on the Hashemis. Our guy says the Little Beirut raid was a mixed bag. Three dead terrorists and no new info."

"But they still won't cut the Hashemis loose?"

Mitch shook his head. "I reached out to Jimbo at the port about the Hashemis' side jobs. Recently, they used Stowe via this woman—

Genie Pullman—to drive out a container they didn't want us to know about."

"Stowe's the union guy, isn't he?"

"Yeah."

"So?"

"Nadia Wright picked up a boyfriend a few months ago. Turns out he lives with Genie Pullman."

"And both of them are gone."

"You got it."

"Grifters."

Mitch nodded.

"And they left the Hashemis holding a bag of piss."

"That's what it looks like."

"You got their pictures?"

"I can get them."

"I want a nice, clean set. There's only so many crooked jewelry dealers who can handle that many diamonds who aren't in our pocket."

"What about the Hashemis?"

"Stay on them. We couldn't find the diamonds at their warehouse. Maybe they were conned or maybe they just want us to think they were conned. I'm going to know one way or the other."

LATE THAT DAY, the Travelers checked into a Quality Inn at a freeway interchange outside Cincinnati, Ohio. The parking lot was half empty. A mom ushered two toddlers down the hall as Danny and Genie made their way to their room. They'd been crisscrossing the country, moving randomly north and south but always west ever since they'd left Point Jericho. Now they were confident that they were completely in the clear. The cartel and the FBI couldn't possibly know where they were.

Danny dropped their overnight bag on the bed nearest the door and kicked off his shoes. "My back teeth are floating."

"Too late." Genie pushed by him and disappeared into the bathroom.

He paced the length of the room, waiting for her to finish. "Time to dial for dollars."

"Who do you want to start with?" she replied.

"Clarence is in Louisville."

Genie came out of the bathroom.

Danny went in.

Genie opened their overnight bag and got out one of the prepaid cellphones they'd bought at a Walmart. She activated it, laid it on the bed, got out her smartphone, input the password for their cloud storage, and found the list of jewelry wholesalers they'd worked with in the past. Danny flushed and came out of the bathroom.

"You're up." Genie handed him the prepaid phone and read off Clarence's phone number.

The phone rang four, five, six times. As Danny was about to hang up, a voice came on the line. "Who's calling?"

"Looking for Clarence."

"And?"

"It's the Traveling Man."

"What was your name the last time we did business?"

Danny thought back. Jesus, when was that? It was before the Seanboro job. "Kevin."

"No disrespect. I had to ask because no one uses this number anymore."

"No problem. You want to do some business?"

"You're persona non grata, my friend. Cartel people came by showing your pictures with the names Danny Briggs and Genie Pullman."

"You're passing up a lot of money."

"Whatever you did, you really pissed them off. Nobody is going to want to touch what you've got. Nobody who wants to live."

"Another time, then."

"Another time."

Danny ended the call. There was no reason for Clarence to

protect them. He pulled the chip from the phone, snapped it in half, and tossed the phone onto the bed.

"That bad?"

"Cartel is circulating pictures of us."

She looked at the list on her smartphone. "What about Lubitz? He's not afraid of anyone."

"I'd rather not. He drives a hard bargain. Still, it could be a good way to find out how bad our situation really is."

He got out another prepaid phone and activated it. Genie read off the phone number. He put the phone on speaker.

"Yeah?"

"Lubitz?"

"Don't say another word. I got a call from a friend before you-know-who got here with your pictures." Lubitz hung up.

Danny pulled the chip from that phone and tossed the phone on the bed beside the first one.

"Call Billy?" Genie asked.

Danny nodded. He made the call from his smartphone. Billy answered on the second ring. Danny put his phone on speaker and explained the problem.

"Yeah," Billy said, "I heard a little chatter. There's a guy in Chicago might be able to help, but he's not exactly trustworthy."

"And that's different how?"

"This guy rides the edge. He'll do everything he can to try to cheat you. There's been talk that he's police protected."

"Will he try to kill us?"

"No, never has."

"Rob us?"

"Anything just shy of that."

"Great. What's his name?"

"Jackson Kennedy. You got a paper and pen?"

Danny leaned over the note pad on the nightstand. "Shoot."

Billy gave him a phone number. "I'm not kidding. Anybody else first."

"Gotcha."

"Maybe you'd be better off stashing the diamonds for a while."

"You need your ten percent, and we need real money to run."

"True enough. Good luck."

Danny put his phone in his pocket.

"What do you think?" Genie asked.

"I think that Lubitz doesn't scare, and he's scared. That anyone too stupid not to be scared is too stupid to deal with. This Kennedy guy, on the other hand, sounds like just the sort of tricky rat bastard who could pull this off. So I guess we're going to Chicago."

"You want me inside or outside of the play."

"We'll figure it out along the way. Right now, we need a decent meal and a good night's sleep."

11

LOOSE ENDS

The next afternoon, MacBurn, Johnston, Lang, and Darrel and his cousins were in the barn at the Lang farm making the final preparations. They were all dressed in work clothes and boots. The three vans were parked facing the barn doors. Each contained four barrels of diesel fuel surrounded by bags of ammonium nitrate fertilizer. The box of depleted uranium, the blasting caps, the C-4, and the remote-control triggers were all laid out on a long folding table. Johnston was putting on a hazmat suit to deal with the uranium.

"Where'd you get the suit?" Lang asked.

"Buddy of mine with Fire & Rescue in Degas County."

"What did you tell him?"

"Didn't have to tell him anything. We grew up together."

MacBurn looked over at Darrel and his cousins. "Nothing to worry about, fellas. Ray will take care of the dangerous part. Then we'll pair up and drive out. Two days from now, we'll all come home and go about our business like we haven't got a clue. And twenty years from now, you'll be bragging to your grandkids about how you helped save this country."

Darrel and his cousins glanced at each other and chuckled nervously.

Lang felt his smartphone vibrate in his pocket. That was the signal. He moved away from the group as if he needed to look inside the nearest van. Explosions blew holes through the walls on either side of the barn, and FBI agents in tactical gear swarmed in.

"On the ground, now!" Agent Ables yelled.

Lang ran for the front door. An FBI agent tackled him, wrestled him to the ground as he made a half-hearted attempt to break free, and cuffed his wrists behind his back. Meanwhile, MacBurn pulled a .38 revolver from his jacket pocket and was shot twice in the chest before he could point it at anyone. Johnston knelt in the hazmat suit with his hands behind his head. Darrel and his cousins all ran in different directions, but the agents chased them down in the farm yard and subdued them. A few minutes later, they were all herded together with Lang and ordered to sit on the floor in the barn.

Martinez jogged in, wearing a Kevlar vest over his suit jacket. Ables took off her helmet and motioned to the folding table. "It's all here, boss."

"Casualties?" Martinez asked.

One of the officers checked MacBurn's neck for a pulse and then shook his head.

"He's the only one," Ables said.

"Let's get these guys out of here and set the perimeter for CSI."

"Yes, sir."

Martinez took out his smartphone. "Rafe? We've got the bombs. You can roll up the rest of them."

The FBI agents hustled Lang, Johnston, and Darrel and his cousins out to a waiting van.

"Did the surveillance cameras capture everything?" Ables asked.

"Lang did a great job setting the cameras," Martinez replied. "We've got everything on video."

"The terrorists and the Fatherland Volk. What a coup for the task force."

"We didn't get Khan, but we did pretty well," Martinez replied.

"We stopped a terrorist act."

"Yes, we did. But now we need to work on the paperwork, make sure the chain of evidence is airtight. We don't want any of these guys wriggling out."

"How bad to you want Lang to look?" Ables asked.

"As bad as any of them."

LATER THAT EVENING, in New York state, three miles outside of Saint Regis, a battered Ford Focus sedan pulled to the side of a tree-lined county road behind an old-fashion station wagon. A Native American man, short hair, gray coveralls and a blue jean jacket, a Glock in his right hand, walked back to the Ford. The woman driving the Ford, a grandmotherly type wearing a nurse's outfit, lowered her window. "You're late," the man said.

"Got stuck behind a tractor for a few miles."

"Where is he?"

"In the trunk."

The man nodded. The woman popped the trunk. "It's time," the man said as he walked back to the open trunk.

Khan, dressed in athletic clothes, his beard barely stubble on his face, climbed out of the trunk and stretched.

"You need help?"

"No," Khan said. He pulled a small black duffel out of the trunk before he lowered the lid.

"Let's go." The man headed back to the station wagon.

Khan stopped at the woman's window, reached into his duffel, and handed her an envelope of cash.

"Thank you," she said.

The man had opened the back of the station wagon to reveal a hidden compartment. "I put a foam pad in there to make it more comfortable."

"This will work?" Khan asked.

"I've been moving cigarettes one way and whiskey the other for over ten years. Piss jug next to the LED lantern. Water bottle in the other corner. Don't mix them up. Your people said you wouldn't be squeamish."

Khan climbed in.

The man closed the cover on the compartment and drove away toward the Canadian border.

FOUR DAYS LATER, Major Tehrani was walking along a path in a city park on his way back to his office after lunch. He wasn't sure how or why Amin Hashemi had been released—no one should have known he was in that lockup—but he would find out. Not that it mattered this time. Zander and Nadia Hashemi had done their part. One World Jihad had picked up the package. He'd received his payment.

As he approached a park bench overlooking a fountain, a man stood up from the bench and turned toward him. Could it be? It was. What was Khan doing here in broad daylight?

"Hello, my friend." Khan stepped in beside him, keeping just far enough away so that no one could be completely sure if they were together.

"You shouldn't be here," Tehrani said.

"I know. I had no choice."

"There is always a choice."

"Some things you have to do yourself."

Khan pulled a syringe from his coat pocket, lurched into Tehrani as if he had stumbled, and injected him in the arm through his jacket.

Tehrani swung around toward him and staggered back. "What have you done?"

"I've paid you back for your carelessness. You should be dead in ten minutes. Of course, such things are imprecise. There's a hospital fifteen minutes away. Maybe you can make it."

"You won't get away with this."

"Your government is going to find evidence that you were working for the Americans. So whatever you've told them about me will be discredited. It's a shame about your wife. She's done nothing."

Tehrani started running toward the street. He felt dizzy, stumbled.

He looked over his shoulder. Khan was gone. Tehrani turned and stepped off the curb. He didn't see the car in time.

GARCIA AND VICTOR were standing on the mall in Washington, DC, nearby the Smithsonian building. Families, foreign tourists, school bus loads of children were in motion all around them.

"Nice work," Garcia said. "The only way it could have turned out better was if we could have turned one of the terrorists."

Victor shrugged.

"You can publicize the Fatherland Volk bust any way you want, but the jihadi takedown has to stay quiet."

"Are you kidding me?"

"We've got agents in the field," Garcia replied. "They need to be protected. You remember Tehrani?"

"The Iranian colonel who used Hashemi and Wright to move the uranium?"

"He's dead."

"Jesus."

"We think Khan had something to do with it."

"So you think he'll want payback all the way down the line."

"I don't know."

"Thanks for the heads-up on this one."

"We'll be in touch."

LATER THAT AFTERNOON, Danny and Genie pulled their stolen Honda into a rest stop on Interstate 80 just east of Chicago. After they heard the bad news in Cincinnati, they'd meandered across Ohio and Indiana, staying in out-of-the-way motels and eating in Mom-and-Pop diners, checking and rechecking for anyone who might be tracking them. Right now they felt just as safe as they could feel with ten million in stolen diamonds and a price on their heads. The parking in front of the welcome center was completely full, people hustling in and out of the building. As Danny slowed down, a minivan backed out of a space and drove away. He pulled in.

"Back in a flash."

He pulled open the glass door, wove his way around two families in front of the first bank of vending machines, and strolled past the door to the men's restroom to find the payphone. He called Kennedy's number. He and Genie had made up their minds. They weren't going to fool around or pretend; they were going to play the hard game of running straight up the field.

"Hello?"

"Jackson Kennedy?"

"Who is this?"

"Danny Briggs. I'm sure you've heard of me."

"I have."

Danny could hear the pleasure in his voice. "I've got something to sell."

"I bet you do."

"You interested in doing business?"

"That depends. You know I've got to have my way, particularly in a situation like this?"

"I do. I'm not expecting the moon, but I am expecting a fair price."

"My warehouse is at the Prairie View office park. There's a back office where the microscope and scales are set up to examine the merchandise."

"I've got another place in mind."

"I'm sure you do, but you know I'm not going there."

"Ditto."

"That makes it hard to get together."

"I'm still a little way out of town. Let me call you back when I get there."

"Okie dokie."

Danny pushed out the doors into the night. Genie was sitting behind the wheel of the Honda. A scan of the parking lot told him there was nothing for him to worry about. Just civilians going about their business. He climbed in the passenger's side.

"Well?"

"We're batting it back and forth. He wants me to come to his warehouse."

"That would be a tough spot."

"No doubt. But he didn't hang up, so he's definitely interested."

"Greedy bastard."

"Yep. Maybe that can work for us. We need to find out more about the lay of the land."

"What about Bobby G? Is he out of prison? He knows about everything happening in the city."

"How do we find him?"

"I think I've still got his ex-wife's phone number."

"That's right. You were friends."

"Friends? I just felt sorry for her."

Genie backed out of their parking space and started toward the freeway entrance. "I can check my laptop to see if I have her number after we get to the motel."

"We could still run. Put the diamonds in a safety deposit box."

She shook her head. "We've got to get rid of the diamonds sooner or later. Might as well be now."

"That's what I think, too. I just wanted to hear you say it."

She pressed on the accelerator as they barreled down the ramp. "Jackson Kennedy is going to play nice. He just doesn't know it yet."

MEANWHILE, the Hashemis—Nadia, Zander, his wife Bonnie, and his daughter Tracy—were staying in a furnished rental house one hundred miles away from Point Jericho. Tracy was back in her bedroom, streaming cartoons on her iPad. Agents Martinez and Ables stood facing Zander, Bonnie, and Nadia in the living room.

"So you're saying we can't go home?" Zander said.

"We're still not sure if it's safe," Martinez said.

"Why would the terrorists be after us?" Zander asked. "It looks like we handed off the package like we were supposed to and then we were arrested, just like everyone else."

"Tehrani's dead. He was murdered on the street in Iran. There's reason to believe the terrorists thought he was responsible for blowing their cover."

"But that doesn't mean they think we had anything to do with it," Zander said.

Bonnie cut in. "We need to go home. We've been gone too long. Tracy misses her friends. She should be in school."

"Maybe after the grand jury testimony. If things have settled down," Martinez said.

"When's that?" Bonnie asked.

"Two more weeks."

"Are we under arrest?"

"No."

"Then you can't keep us here. We can go home whenever we want."

"And you'll take your lives into your hands. We can't protect you there."

"What about Danny?" Nadia asked. "Have you found him?"

"I told you. He and his partner disappeared. We don't need them for this case, so we're not going to devote resources to finding them."

"So you've got no idea where they are?"

"Our only concern is to keep you safe."

"And we have to stay here two more weeks?"

"Maybe less. We'll see. Look, we've got to go. If you need anything, just tell the agents outside. I'll be in touch if anything changes."

Martinez and Ables walked down the sidewalk toward their Ford Explorer. Ables waved at the two agents sitting in the Camry parked at the curb.

"They are a needy bunch," Ables said.

"Not used to not having their own way."

"I'd be happy to cut them loose, if that's what they want."

"After the grand jury," Martinez said. "Their testimony won't be used at trial, but I want the jury to have the complete picture of what the Fatherland Volk was up to, which means the jihadi connection.

And it will give us a little more time to judge what's happening with the terrorists."

They climbed into their Ford Explorer, Ables behind the wheel.

Martinez put on his seatbelt. "Do we actually have any new info on Briggs and Pullman?"

"Nothing, boss. There haven't been any hits from the database. You going to tell Nadia that she was probably being played?"

"And make her angry or ashamed? I'm not going to tell her anything that might upset her and affect her cooperation."

"But she ought to know."

"Not my problem."

BONNIE LOCKED the door behind the FBI agents. "Well, that was a waste of time. This is exactly why people won't come forward to help the police. You get jerked around like you were a criminal."

"It is a pain in the butt," Zander said. "But I can understand their point of view. If we were murdered—"

"That's just so much BS," Bonnie replied. "All you did was report some terrorists who wanted to use you."

"We do need to get back to business," Nadia said. "Our bills aren't paying themselves."

"I thought you said we had enough money in the bank to weather this?" Zander asked.

"We do. I didn't mean it like that."

"I'm going to check on Tracy," Bonnie said.

As soon as Bonnie disappeared down the hall, Nadia took Zander by the arm and pulled him into the kitchen. She whispered. "We don't know what happened to the diamonds."

"Mr. Wishes isn't going to contact us as long as the FBI are around."

"So does the cartel have the diamonds? Are we in the clear? Or are they getting angrier by the day?"

He glanced out into the living room to make sure Bonnie hadn't come back. "You think that the cartel is a bigger threat than the terrorists?"

"Tehrani's dead. Also the guy who came for the package. Do the other terrorists even know who we are? I'm not much concerned about them anymore, but I'd sleep a lot better if the cartel had their diamonds."

"At least Danny got away."

"Yeah, that's something. He told me they'd run. Wanted us to do the same. I wish there was a way he could get in touch."

AFTER DANNY and Genie checked in to a Budget Inn on the outskirts of Chicago, Genie got out her laptop and searched her encrypted cloud storage, where she found a phone number for Bobby G's ex-wife. Three rings later, she had a phone number for Bobby G.

"Think this number's any good?"

"The man mistreats her every day, and she's still waiting for his call. I bet the number's good."

Danny called the phone number.

"Yeah?"

"Hey, brother."

"Trav, how you doing? You lining up a job?"

"I don't know yet. I need info on a guy in your playground. Jackson Kennedy."

"Kennedy? That dude thinks he's a bad man. Got a reputation for hard bargaining. But he's never dropped any bodies, far as I know."

"Do you know where his warehouse is?"

"Warehouse? He's got a building in the Prairie View office park, but I wouldn't call it a warehouse. Let me look it up." He gave Danny an address.

"Thanks, Bobby."

"No sweat. Keep me in mind if you're lining up anything."

"You bet."

Genie opened the property search feature in the county assessor's website. The property description for the building indicated three offices in the back, a kitchen, two washrooms, and a large open area in front.

"The inside of the building is doable," Danny said.

Genie clicked over to the GPS view. The GPS showed a treeless lot, asphalt parking, and a metal building that had probably been some sort of factory at one time.

He pointed at the laptop screen. "Widen out."

She zoomed out to show the nearby buildings. "Lots of space. No good sniping angles."

"Yeah. Almost too good to be true. What do you think?"

"Plenty of privacy to make a deal or do an ambush."

"But he's a middleman, not a killer. A hard bargainer, not a straight-up thief. He's out of business if people think he'll break a deal."

"But who is his deal with? Us or somebody else?"

Danny laughed. "He'll be in the kill box with us."

"I know. I'm just saying we'll need a backup plan."

"Honey, we always need a backup plan."

"Make the call."

He got out a new prepaid phone, input Kennedy's phone number, and put the phone on speaker. "I'm back."

"Change your mind?"

"Your building that little place on the east side in that business park?"

"You're doing your homework."

"Let's have a meet."

"How about tomorrow at ten o'clock?"

"Ten o'clock it is."

"It'll be me, my bodyguard, and my diamond guy."

"It'll just be the two of us. We'll be armed."

"Of course. See you tomorrow."

Danny ended the call and pulled the chip from the phone.

"Do you still need to do that?" Genie asked.

"Are the cops on him? Are his offices bugged? Is the cartel waiting around the corner? Just seems like a reasonable amount of precaution."

THE NEXT MORNING at 9:45 a.m., Danny and Genie pulled into the parking lot of Kennedy's building in a freshly stolen Ford Escape and parked facing out at the north exit. A black BMW was parked at the front by the doors. At 10:00 a.m., a skinny man whose beer belly was bulging out of his gray suit jacket and a large bearded man with a shaved head and a pistol holstered at his side came out of the building. Danny and Genie got out of the car and walked toward them.

"Danny and Genie," the skinny man said. "You look exactly like your pictures."

"You must be Jackson Kennedy," Danny replied.

"Got the diamonds?"

"Got the cash?"

"Come on inside."

The bodyguard held the door open for them. They walked into a large workspace with loose electrical wires hanging from the ceiling. To one side was a desk with a desktop computer connected to the surveillance cameras on the outside of the building.

"Drake will keep an eye on the perimeter. I had the building swept this morning, so we're all safe."

The bodyguard sat down at the desk. Danny, Genie, and Kennedy continued into the central back office. A six-foot-tall floor safe sat against the right wall. A sofa and two chairs were arranged around a coffee table in the center of the room. At the back, an elderly man with a short goatee sat at a worktable behind a digital scale and a gem microscope. He looked at them, but he didn't say a word.

"Let's get this done," Kennedy said.

Danny handed him the bag of diamonds. He passed it to the elderly man, who set it on the digital scale. "Eight ounces with the bag." The elderly man spoke with a slight European accent.

"Have a seat," Kennedy said.

They sat around the coffee table, watching the elderly man as he chose diamonds at random and examined them under the micro-scope. Finally, he looked up.

"These are genuine, of good quality."

"What's the net weight?" Kennedy asked.

"One thousand carats."

"Well, well," Kennedy said.

"That's what?" Danny asked. "Ten million retail?"

"We're a long way from retail, my friend."

"Five hundred thousand."

"You'd be lucky to get two hundred thousand if they didn't belong to the Orange Hill Cartel."

"What's your offer?"

"Seventy thousand."

Danny laughed. "One hundred seventy, you got a deal."

Kennedy shook his head. "These stones—I'm going to have to sit on them half a year and then trickle them out slowly, mixed with other scores. It could take a year to get rid of them. A year my money is tied up. A year I'm at risk from the cartel. No can do. Ninety thousand."

"I don't know why I'm believing your bullshit. One hundred fifteen thousand in old bills right now, and you've got a deal."

"Done."

Kennedy went to the safe, input the code and his fingerprint, opened the heavy door, and counted money off a shelf into a reusable grocery bag. He brought the bag and a money counter back to the coffee table. "Everything above board," he said.

He ran the one hundred dollar bills through the money counter. When the display read "$115,000" he stopped. "It's all there."

Danny turned to Genie. "Check it."

She took a blacklight pen from her pocket and ran it over the one hundred dollar bills at random, checking for the pink line. The money was real.

"Satisfied?" Kennedy asked.

"I'd like more money," Danny replied.

Kennedy chuckled. "You and me both."

Genie put the cash into her shoulder bag. She and Danny stood up.

"Adios," Danny said.

"Do us both a favor," Kennedy replied. "Don't come back this way for a least six months."

Danny and Genie left out the front door. "What do you think?" she asked.

"This deal stinks. He's supposed to be a hard bargainer."

"Yep. He didn't really sweat us, threaten to leave us dangling."

"And this parking lot. His car, our car—it's just too perfect."

"So it's plan B?"

He nodded. They ran across the street to the Winning Ways call center, cut around the far side of the building to the employee parking lot and got into a Toyota 4Runner they'd left among the third-shift cars. Danny drove over the lawn, dropped onto the boule-vard, and stepped on the gas. He ran the first stop sign. "How does it look?"

Genie glanced out the back. "Nothing yet."

At the next intersection, the traffic light was green. Just as they sped through, a blue Audi screeched into the intersection from the right, fishtailed for a couple hundred feet, and began closing in on them. A few careful gunshots punched into the back of the 4Runner.

"Are we going to make it?" Genie asked.

"You bet."

He sped down the boulevard, weaving through the traffic. Genie was turned in her seat, watching the Audi.

"They still back there?" he asked.

"Yeah, but they're too far away to shoot at us. You surprised that Kennedy sold us out?"

"No."

"You think the guys in the Audi are his or the cartel's?"

"Don't have time to think about it. We've got to lose them, either way."

In the business park near Midway airport, he turned into the parking garage at a Marriott Hotel, used the hotel key card to raise the gate, and scooted up through the levels to the top, where he pulled in next to the hotel access door. He swiped the card, the door beeped, and the they were running down the hall toward the interior elevator.

"Think we've lost them?" he asked.

"You know they're going to try to seal the building."

"Stairs or elevator?"

"Elevator is better for us."

They stood in front of the elevator, hands on the pistols in their jacket pockets. As the door opened, they lifted their pistols to fire through their jackets. The elevator was empty. They got in. Genie pressed the mezzanine button. They each stood in a back corner. The elevator dropped through the floors, stopping on the tenth floor to take on a middle-aged couple with two roller bags, and on the fourth floor for a mom with a little girl. They were both going to the lobby.

The door opened at the mezzanine level. Danny and Genie got out, acting as if they were strangers, moving toward the restrooms situated between the meeting rooms. Danny glanced over the railing. A big guy, his hands in the pockets of his coat, lounged by the main entrance. Danny watched Genie go into the ladies' room just before he entered the men's room. Three urinals. Two stalls. Empty. He stood at the sink, took a fake mustache from his pocket, and pushed it into place. A little ridiculous, but at a distance it would work. He wet his hair and combed it down slick on his head. Then he took a nylon jacket from his suitcoat pocket and put it on over his suitcoat.

As Danny turned to leave, the big guy from downstairs pushed into the restroom. Danny shoved his hand into his suit coat pocket to grab his pistol. The big guy dropped into a boxer's crouch, knocked Danny's pistol hand up with his left and punched Danny in the face with his right. Danny shifted his head, caught a glancing blow on his chin, and fell back against the sink, clawing in his pocket for the gun. The guy punched him below the ribs. Danny fell to his hands and knees, spun away from the man, and tried to scramble to his feet.

Just then, the restroom door burst open. Danny glanced over his shoulder. Genie was on the guy's back, clawing at his eyes. The man lurched backward, his hands flying about, trying to knock Genie loose. Danny snapped his lockback knife out of his pants pocket, grabbed the front of the man's jacket, and stabbed the man repeatedly as he used the man's jacket to climb to his feet. Genie rode the man down as he collapsed to the floor.

"The door," Danny said.

Genie jammed the trashcan under the door knob. "You okay?"

"That was close," Danny said.

"You should have shot him."

"I was trying." He looked at the restroom door. "Did you see anyone else?"

"He was the only one."

"Let's clean this up." They muscled the big guy into a stall and left him sitting on the toilet. Then they wiped up the blood smeared across the floor with wet paper towels.

They both turned to the mirror, Genie adjusting her blonde wig and Danny washing his hands before he ran his fingers back through his hair. His nylon shell was splattered with blood.

"That's not going to work," Genie said.

"I know." He pulled off the nylon shell and put it in the trashcan. "At least I still have the mustache. Let's try for the side door by the coffee shop. You first. I'll meet you on the street."

They left the restroom. Danny walked to the elevator and stood there as if he was waiting to go up. Genie glanced over the railing. Three people waiting to check in. One person sitting in the lounging area. No one who looked suspicious. She went down the stairs to the lobby, moving with purpose, keeping close to the wall. A woman and a man, both in business wear, started up the stairs toward her, but they had conference nametags clipped to their suitcoats. She turned left and glanced into the coffee shop. A gaggle of customers were waiting at the counter for their orders, and most of the tables were occupied. She pushed through the side door to the outside and looked up and down the street. Cars were moving in both directions. No one was slowing down. She walked south, away from the hotel, looking at the cars in the on-street parking.

About half a block down the street, she spotted an old Dodge. The parking meter still had an hour on it. She glanced back toward the hotel. Danny was on the sidewalk. She picked the door lock and hotwired the car before Danny caught up to her.

"Good find," he said.

She turned right at the first intersection. "We going for our go-bag?"

"They didn't know about the 4Runner, so the pickup we left on the street with the go-bag in it has got to be in the clear."

"But now the cartel knows where we are."

"Not for long. Nobody's tailing us."

"Wonder what they were paying Kennedy to rat us out?"

"A lot less than the hundred and fifteen thousand we walked away with."

"So we switch to the pickup?"

"Yeah, it'll be good for a couple more days. Where do you want to go on vacation?"

"California."

"North or south?"

"Let's do some wine tasting."

"Wine tasting it is."

12

END GAME

Later that afternoon, Mr. Wishes, dressed in a black suit and overcoat, sat across the desk from Kennedy in Kennedy's office at the Prairie View office park.

"Sorry about your guy," Kennedy said.

"Me too," Mr. Wishes replied.

"Do you know where Briggs and Pullman are?"

"We're going to find out."

"I'm out a hundred and fifteen thousand. Plus I'll have to smooth things over with the cops."

"We appreciate the trouble you've gone to for us. Where are the diamonds?"

"In my safe."

"Let's have them."

"What about my money?"

Mr. Wishes took an envelope from his suitcoat and tossed it onto the desk. Kennedy looked inside. "What's this?"

"It's the finder's fee we promised you."

"Twenty thousand dollars? You must be kidding me. What about my one hundred and fifteen thousand?"

"You're an independent. The deal was twenty thousand and a

favor to be determined later. If you had been with us, you wouldn't have been using your own money. Besides, we don't know what you actually gave them. We just know what we promised you."

"There must be someone else I can talk to."

Mr. Wishes shook his head. "I'm the guy."

"Well, what about my favor for later?"

Mr. Wishes took a .38 revolver from his pocket and rested it on his thigh. "I promise not to kill you if you quit arguing and give me the diamonds. That's as much of a favor as I can promise right now."

Kennedy went to his safe, input the code and thumbprint, and opened the door. He glanced over his shoulder. Mr. Wishes was standing with his revolver pointed at him. "What's this?"

"Some people keep a loaded gun in their safe. Some people don't think too clearly when they've lost money."

Kennedy grabbed the bag of diamonds and closed the safe. "I'm not crazy, okay? I don't want you people after me."

"Wise decision."

Kennedy handed him the bag of diamonds.

Mr. Wishes weighed the bag in his hand. "They're all here?"

"I can call my guy to come in and weigh them if you like."

Mr. Wishes put the revolver in his suitcoat pocket and the diamonds in his overcoat pocket. "See you around."

Kennedy followed him out to the front door and locked it behind him. Goddamn, he thought. I should have kept my mouth shut. I should have just made the deal and kept the diamonds.

A WEEK LATER, back in Point Jericho, Mr. Wishes sat with Mitch in the back booth of a poorly lit bar across the street from a strip club. Mitch took a pull off his bottle of beer. "The Hashemis got back in town today. What do you want to do about them?"

"What's their situation?"

"Our inside guy says the conspiracy charges were dropped. Their lawyer convinced the cops that they didn't know about the terrorist package. At least, that's what they're saying. It seems a little fishy to me."

"Well, they're out of the smuggling business. Cops will be all over them from here on out. So they're of no use to us in the future."

"But they were in with the grifters who stole the diamonds."

"Were they? The grifters ran out on them. We got the diamonds back. Did they snitch on us to cut a deal?"

"No."

"So how does killing them help us? All it will do is draw the cops down on us."

Mitch nodded. "If they weren't in with the grifters."

"They're going to get in touch. As soon as I talk to them I'll know if they're players or if they were played."

Mr. Wishes looked down the bar. A Latino wearing a tan overcoat was standing at the bar with one foot on the rail. "Anything else? I've got business to attend to."

Mitch slid out of the booth. The Latino took his spot. "What have you got for me?" Mr. Wishes asked.

"We found the pickup the grifters drove out of Chicago. It was parked at a Target outside Denver. From there—nothing. Nothing on any of the surveillance cameras in the area, nothing at any nearby motels or restaurants."

"Keep branching out from there."

"Will do."

"They're got to be somewhere."

AFTER ZANDER and Nadia dropped Bonnie and Tracy off at home, they drove out to the Hashemi Carpets & Arts building. The parking lot was empty and junk mail was hanging out of the mailbox. Inside the warehouse, they had expected to see three rolled carpets still on the worktable where they'd left them and the four pallets of rolled carpets, one pallet almost emptied. But now the fourth pallet had partially unwrapped carpets dumped haphazardly all around it, and off on the other side of the room, they found the unrolled carpet with the slit-open diamond bag. "What a disaster," Nadia said.

"Mr. Wishes must have found the diamonds," Zander replied.

"They sure made a mess."

Zander got down on his knees and started peeling the tape from the edges of the black bag. "I'm going to call in some of the guys to clean things up and get the inventory sorted out."

"You'll have to start from scratch."

"I know."

"I'll get started on the office work," Nadia said.

"You know we've got to call Mr. Wishes. Make sure the cartel knows we can't help them anymore."

"Do we have to do that today? It's not going to be a fun conversation."

"You know how touchy he is," Zander said. "We don't want him thinking we're disrespecting him. We just got out of trouble. We don't want to get back in."

"You're right."

"Listen. I'll call the guys, see who can come in today, at least get them back on schedule, then I'll go to the payphone at the truck stop and call Mr. Wishes. You work with the guys until I get back."

"Okay."

An hour later, Zander was standing at one of the payphones in front of the restrooms at the Lazy 8 truck stop. The truck stop was busy with the dinner crowd. The dining room tables were full and the convenience store area was crowded with travelers stocking up on snacks and drinks. He input Mr. Wishes's phone number.

"Hello?"

"It's Zander."

"Where are you calling from?"

"Payphone."

"I was wondering when you'd get in touch."

"I thought we better talk."

"Not on the phone. Tomorrow. At the cemetery. Same place as before. You remember?"

"Yes."

"Eleven o'clock. Bring your sister."

"Why?"

"Not on the phone. Eleven a.m." Mr. Wishes ended the call.

Zander hung up the phone and made his way around the people clustered at the checkout. Something wasn't right. There was too much menace in his voice. He glanced around in the parking lot. Was someone following him? How would he know? Everyone just looked like they were going about their business. He drove back to the warehouse. Two of their employees were already there, helping Nadia to recheck the carpets they had already checked before the FBI took them into protective custody. They were refolding a ten-by-twelve carpet so that they could reroll it.

"Nadia," he said, "Can I talk to you a second?"

They walked out of earshot of their employees. Zander told her what had happened. "What does it mean?" she asked.

"I don't know."

"Well, we have to go."

"Yeah."

"Talking about it won't change that."

"No."

"We're just going to tell the truth."

"It's all we can do."

She handed him the clipboard. "How late do you want to stay today?"

"A couple of hours should make a good start."

"I'll be in the office."

AT ELEVEN O'CLOCK the next morning, Zander and Nadia were parked on the side of the asphalt roadway on the hill in Point Jericho Memorial Cemetery where Zander had parked before. Up the hill, near a cedar tree, they could see Mr. Wishes standing at the headstone, waiting patiently. "Let me talk first," Zander said. "These conversations have a rhythm. We want to get in, get out, and get on with our lives."

"You look scared."

"I am scared. I'm always scared when I meet him. He's a scary guy."

They walked up the hill to the grave where Mr. Wishes stood waiting with his gloved hands clasped in front of him. Their shoes left prints in the light dusting of snow that had fallen overnight. When Zander and Nadia stepped up beside him, Mr. Wishes turned his head.

"Right on time. I've always liked that about you."

Zander opened his mouth to speak, but before he could say anything, Mr. Wishes continued. "And you must be the lovely Nadia Wright."

She nodded.

"Do you two know why you're here?"

"We warned you about the FBI," Zander said.

"Yes, you did."

"And you got the diamonds."

"Yes. But do you know how?"

"You took them from the warehouse."

"No." Mr. Wishes pivoted to look at both of them, his hands still clasped together. "Your friends Danny and Genie took them."

Zander's face turned gray. Nadia's eyes went blank, and her jaw started working as if she were chewing on something she couldn't swallow.

"But," Zander said, "you said you had them."

"Oh yes."

Nadia's mind flashed to the last time she and Danny were together, the sound of his voice, the touch of his hands on her skin, that feeling of complete intimacy in the moment right after when they were still locked together. Her stomach rolled over. It had all been a lie.

"Is he dead?" she asked.

"Not yet."

"What do you want with us?" Zander asked. "We can't smuggle for you anymore."

"I haven't made a decision."

"We didn't know."

"I believe you, but that's not the point. The point is, can we trust you moving forward?"

"We didn't tell the FBI anything about the diamonds."

"I know. But we still have to decide what we're going to do."

Mr. Wishes walked off over the hill.

Zander put his hand on Nadia's shoulder. "What a mess."

"I don't want to talk about it."

"At least we're not dead."

"Not yet."

A FEW DAYS LATER, while Nadia was tidying up her townhouse, she found a shirt that belonged to Danny lying in the bottom of her bedroom closet. She pulled the crumpled shirt up to her face, inhaled Danny's scent, and then held the shirt to her chest. It had always been too good to be true. If she hadn't fooled herself, if she hadn't been so needy, she'd have seen right through him. She carried the shirt through to the kitchen and put it in the trash. The love affair, the help with the special package, it was all designed to put her and Zander at ease and put them out of the way so that Danny and Genie could rip off the cartel. They didn't care at all what might happen to her or Zander if the diamonds were stolen from their warehouse.

She frowned. He had warned her, though. He had told her to make her own escape plan, not to rely on the FBI to protect them. And putting the FBI in the picture had probably saved their lives. If they'd been there that afternoon without the diamonds, Mr. Wishes would have killed them on the spot. Instead, he found out that Danny and Genie were responsible, that she and Zander had been duped, too. Had Danny planned it that way? Had he tried, in his own selfish way, to keep her safe?

Not that is mattered now. She and Zander weren't going to run.

This was their town. This is where their business was. Besides, there was no place where the cartel couldn't find them. If they wanted to kill them, they could do it at will. Her smartphone rang. It was Zander. "Yeah?"

"I talked to the guy."

"Which guy?"

"The guy. The one who matters."

"Why did you do that?"

"I had to try. I just couldn't wait and hope anymore. I wanted to make plans for Bonnie and Tracy if I had to."

"And?"

"We've got nothing to worry about as long as we keep quiet and stay out of their way."

"You're serious?"

"Yep."

"And that's all?"

The line was quiet for a moment. "We owe them a favor. One to be determined later."

"That sounds more like it."

"It's still a relief."

"You're not kidding." She glanced out the kitchen window into the backyard. The neighbor kids were out on their play structure. "So we're done with Tehrani and the cartel."

"Thank God. No more smuggling."

"That's for sure." She watched a little girl slide down the slide. "Hey, how are things with Tracy?"

"Don't get me started. She's still not talking to me except when she yells. Why did she miss Rachel's party? Why does she have three weeks of school work to make up?"

"She'll get over it."

"Can't be soon enough."

"And Bonnie?"

"That's more complicated. She still doesn't quite believe that we got into this problem so innocently."

"But things are going better?"

"Yeah. It'll just take time."

"Well, it all worked out, crazy as it was. We're still in business, and you've still got your family."

"I know. And you've got me."

"I know."

"Listen, Sis, I'm not blaming you for Danny. We both know I didn't trust him, especially in the beginning, but he was looking more and more like he might work out. Couldn't take Pauly's place, of course, but I knew you needed someone, that I needed to mind my own business. So he fooled me, too."

"Thanks for saying that, Zander. See you tomorrow."

She looked back out the window over the sink. The kids were playing tag. The neighbor woman came to her back door and called them. The bird feeder was empty, and the neighbor's cat was prowling through the back shrubs. Their lives had almost been ruined. It would be easy to blame Tehrani or the cartel or Danny and Genie. But she and Zander had played their part by being greedy and stupid. Now they had a second chance. She should have felt happy, but her heart was broken. She needed to cry, cry away the sorrow of being fooled instead of loved, but she just couldn't do it. Not yet. All she could do was put one foot in front of the other.

She turned on the faucet, wet the sponge, and wiped the counter. She was hungry. She needed to eat. Should she go out or order in?

JOE LANG WAS SITTING on the porch glider at the Lang farm outside Summerville. His cheek was still bruised from a jail fight the week before. It was unusually warm afternoon for late October, and he was enjoying the heat on his face. In theory, he was out on bail awaiting trial for aiding and abetting a terrorist act. The DA bought his story that he was coerced, or so she said. But the truth was that Martinez had arranged the whole thing, hoping to leverage the bombing case into an opportunity to infiltrate more cells of the Fatherland Volk, something the FBI had not be able to do so far.

As he was watching a hawk swoop down into the cut hayfield, he noticed the dust cloud of a vehicle speeding down the gravel road toward him. As it got closer, he saw that it was a black Chevy truck he'd never seen before. He picked up the Glock lying on the seat beside him and chambered a round.

The truck turned up onto his gravel driveway and came to a stop. A lanky blond man with an SS tattoo on his neck got out. His hands were in the pockets of his barn coat. "Hey," he said.

"Can I help you? There's nothing else out on this road."

"You Joe Lang?"

He nodded.

"Some mutual friends sent me to see about you."

"That so? How do I know you're not a cop?"

"You don't. How'd you get out on bail?"

"Johnston didn't talk. Feds got no evidence of me actually doing anything except being here. My lawyer thinks I'll do all right."

He smiled. "We heard Johnston is about to break."

"I don't believe it."

"Feds are going to make him a deal so that his wife doesn't lose his military pension."

"That's bullshit."

"Maybe. You want to take that chance or do you want to stay free?"

"How's that?"

"You get in the truck with me now. You never come back. We've got places where a true believer can keep on living."

"Why should I trust you?"

"Suit yourself. It's your life."

Lang studied the man as if he was trying to make up his mind. Then he nodded. "You want something to drink?"

"You got a beer?"

"Come on up."

The man climbed up the steps to the porch. Lang came back out with a bottle of beer. "Give me a few minutes to pack."

"You bet." The man sat down.

Later that evening, when he was in a restroom stall at a rest stop,

Lang texted Martinez. *I'm inside. I'm ditching this phone. I'll be in touch in a week.*

Two weeks later, the Travelers, now going by the names Roger and Leena Belmont, were sitting in recliners under a poolside umbrella at a resort in Napa Valley, California. A dozen people were around the pool, sunning themselves, reading, splashing in the water. Leena sipped her Bloody Mary, while Roger slathered on sunscreen.

"What do you want to do about Kennedy?" Leena asked.

"You keep on coming back to him."

"He's a loose end."

"He sold us out, but we escaped, and we got his money," Roger said.

"So he gets a pass?"

"I didn't say that. In six months or a year—when we're sure the Orange Hill Cartel isn't nosing around—maybe we could go back and crack his safe." Roger put down the sunscreen and sat back in his recliner. "All in all, that job worked out just fine."

"Except when it didn't."

"There were a few tight places."

"Tight places? You almost got killed at the hotel."

"But I didn't."

"And you were a little too generous with Nadia."

"Yeah, but it didn't seem that way at the time. I guess she pulled at my heart a little. She was so sweet and trusting. Maybe because I reminded her of her dead husband."

"Maybe."

"Didn't stop us from taking the diamonds, though, did it? Besides, we don't jam up other players unless they're got it coming, and Nadia and her brother were two of the most clueless amateur criminals we've seen in a long time."

"Think the cartel will kill them?"

"Don't have any idea. Hope not. Wouldn't serve any purpose."

"Well, I think they're going to manage to wriggle out." She waved at a server making his way among the recliners. "I'm getting another Bloody Mary. Want anything?"

"Lunch menu."

"Wouldn't you rather put on a shirt and go into the restaurant?"

"No, I want to take advantage of this heat wave. Let's just sit here and relax."

A NOTE FROM THE AUTHOR

Thanks for reading *Thicker Than Thieves*. If you enjoyed it, please post a short review on a review site of your choice. A few words will do. Honest reviews are the number one way I attract new readers.

Thanks so much.

I'd love to hear from you. You can reach me at my website: https://michaelpking.org

The Travelers
The Double Cross: A Travelers Prequel
The Traveling Man: Book One
The Computer Heist: Book Two
The Blackmail Photos: Book Three
The Freeport Robbery: Book Four
The Kidnap Victim: Book Five
The Murder Run: Book Six
The Casino Switcheroo: Book Seven
Thicker Than Thieves: Book Eight

www.ingramcontent.com/pod-product-compliance
Lightning Source LLC
Chambersburg PA
CBHW032134170626
46808CB00006B/2230